Called by the Bear
Book 3

Cover by Croco Designs
Editing by Jodi Henley and Red Adept Publishing

Called by the Bear

Book 3

V. VAUGHN

PART 1

CHAPTER 1

Taylor

GREAT. A LARGE pair of boobs walk toward me, and I hold back my groan when I realize who it is. Judging from the blue eyes that are like Carly's, it's my next appointment, Lucy Robichaux. She must have thought Taylor was a guy, because she's dressed for bouncing and jiggling, not a workout.

"Hey, Lucy, I'm Taylor."

A hint of pink flushes her cheeks as she says, "Oh." She puts her hands on her hips and assesses me. "You're the great warrior trainer for the Le Roux?"

I've gone from a martial arts enthusiast to a kick-ass werebear warrior since I answered the call of the bear and moved to Maine. "I am." Seriously, I have to prove myself to this bimbo? I let my gaze roam up and down her body. "You might want to put on something more appropriate."

She squints at me. "I don't take shit from people like you." She turns and starts to walk away.

Crap. *Where did that come from?* I know better than

to embarrass a client. "Wait. I've got a shirt you can wear."

She stops and stands still with her back to me. I say, "Look, we started on the wrong foot. I know your mother really wants you to train with us, and my alpha insisted you have the best."

She turns around and tilts her head to the side. "You're the best?"

"Yup." I walk over to the shelves on the wall, and the plastic is slick in my hand when I grab the handles of a jump rope. "So what do you say? Want to learn how to kick butt?"

Anger flickers in her eyes before she hides it with a shrug. "Whatever."

"Warm up with this while I go find you a T-shirt." Using my bear strength I toss the jump rope at her. I wince when it makes my low-grade headache flare. I need some ibuprofen.

Lucy's reflexes are quick, and she snatches it out of the air. The rope slaps in staccato against the hard rubber floor as she jumps, and I make my way over to the office I share with Ian.

He's grinning when I walk in. "I'm going to guess you've forgotten your education at charm school."

I snort, and the contents of a drawer rattle when I yank it open in search of medication. "Very funny. Careful or I'll make you train her."

"Oh, no. That princess is all yours." Ian opens another drawer, grabs a white plastic bottle, and pops off the top. "Still got that headache?"

"Yeah. I can't seem to shake it." I grab my morning mug of tea from our desk and take a swig to wash down two blue pills. The drink is nasty when it's hot and even worse when it's cold. But I need to consume the whole thing, so I shudder swallowing it all. "Think her brother is a dick?" He's booked for my afternoon session.

Ian crosses his arms, and his chair squeaks as he leans back. "Doesn't matter if he is, you'll put him in his place in a matter of seconds."

I roll my eyes at him and turn to the shelves of black Kick It logo T-shirts. The cotton is soft in my fingers as I search for the right size. I got my period this morning, and I feel like taking out my disappointment on everyone around me.

Ian says, "Your hidden ability is pretty impressive. But I bet it didn't get you many dates."

"It's a gift, and besides, I was waiting for my true mate all these years."

"Ouch."

Crap on a cracker. Ian's dating Annie, whose true mate died, while Ian hasn't found his yet. It's a touchy subject. "I'm sorry. I didn't mean that."

The wheels of his chair roll across the vinyl tile with a hum as he tucks himself into the desk again to straighten a pile of papers. "S'cool. I'm just giving you shit."

"Yeah, but I don't know what's gotten into me. I'm not usually a mean person."

Ian stands to come toward me. "No. You're not.

You've put in a lot of hours over the past month. Maybe you need to take a few days off."

Opening up the Kick It martial arts studio has taken up most of my time, but not enough to keep me from pursuing my real dream—having Keith's children. Unfortunately I can't seem to get pregnant, and it's not for lack of trying.

"I can't. I've got—"

Ian's hands land heavy on my shoulders, and his kind eyes gaze down at me. "Nothing I can't handle. After Lucy, go home, and get some sleep. If you don't feel better tomorrow, don't come in."

I step out from under the weight that brings the bone-deep ache I'm feeling to the surface. I glance out to see Lucy stretching. "Let me see how this morning goes. But I might take you up on that offer."

Ian rubs his hands together. "I wouldn't mind having a crack at that cocky Luke Robichaux." He shadowboxes a bit. "Maybe knock him down a peg or two."

I grin at him. "Now who needs charm school?"

Two hours later I'm drenched in sweat, and my body feels as if I ran a marathon. I must be coming down with something, because my workout with Lucy was an easy one. While she's quick on her feet, she's not in great shape, and I shouldn't feel as if I barely kept up.

Ian hands me my sweatshirt. "You look like shit. Go home."

Lifting the thick cotton over my head makes my arms tremble. "I feel like it. Thanks for covering for me."

"No problem."

Using my whole body I push myself out the door and into sunlight so bright it sends shooting pain through my head. All I want to do is get in my car and get home, but I need my fertility tea. I make my way down the block to Earth Elements.

I enter a small dark shop and am immediately overwhelmed by the aroma of incense. It makes my stomach lurch, and I swallow down bile before I call out. "Nina?"

"Taylor." The cool hand of a petite girl touches my arm. The vision of an old man flashes in my mind, and I shake my head to clear it as she says, "Wow, you look awful." A hopeful smile covers her face. "Are you pregnant?"

I sigh. "No. But I'm sick and on my way home. I stopped by for the tea blend you made me."

Nina moves behind the counter and grabs a bag from a shelf. "It's all set. Let me add something to boost your immune system too."

My stomach rolls, and if I have to stay here much longer I'm going to vomit all over the floor. Closing my eyes, I will myself to keep it together, but the toothless smile of my previous vision fills my head. "Sure."

When I open them again Nina shoves the bag into my hands. "I have your card on file. Go."

I offer a smile. "Thanks."

"Take care of yourself." Her voice fades as I walk out the door she holds open for me. My skin moistens with a slick coat of sweat as I make my way toward my truck, and I open my jacket to let the cold in. A cackling laughter I swear is from the old man in my mind makes me turn to see if he's behind me, but nobody is there. Great, my fever must be so high I'm hallucinating.

The cold leather of the car seat soothes my overheated body, and sunglasses help with the pounding in my head. Cracking my window open, I welcome the cool breeze that comes in as I drive home. My stomach has settled, and even my headache is almost gone by the time I get home.

I park in the driveway and get out of my truck. My sneakers tap lightly on frozen asphalt as I walk to the mailbox. It occurs to me that maybe I am pregnant. Now that I think about it, I've been nauseated most mornings for a while now. And it fades by evening. The metal flap screeches when I open it to retrieve letters and flyers. Hope blossoms in me because it is possible to bleed after conception. I imagine how happy Keith would be if I were carrying his children.

It's been hard to see Carly and Sierra each day. They talk about their babies, and while I'm happy for them, I'm also jealous. Once I'm in the house I go straight to the kitchen to put my tea in the cabinet for tomorrow morning. I toss the mail, and it slaps down on the counter. A cooking magazine slides out from the pile. A stir-fry dish is on the cover, and it appears so appetizing my mouth waters.

I grab the magazine to read and settle into the couch for a nap. Scanning the vegetable dish recipe makes me decide I'll cook a healthy dinner tonight, because if I'm pregnant I'm going to need the nutrients for our babies. Closing my eyes, I lay my hands on my belly and envision my favorite fantasy. I fall asleep with children's laughter ringing in my mind.

CHAPTER 2

Carly

B RADY'S WARM FINGERS wrap around my hand. "I can't believe I'm alone with you."

The engine of our Hummer revs as we begin to climb a steep hill. We're on our way to dinner at the Robichaux's, and they live on Herman Mountain.

I give my husband a squeeze. "I know. I've been thinking and have decided we need to book a date night each week."

It's a full moon, and the night sky is bright. Brady winks at me. "You mean like the dates we used to have?"

I chuckle as I recall we only had one date, although it was a memorable one. I almost shot Keith when he shifted, was unofficially married, slept with Brady, and when he bit me, I accidentally changed into a werebear. "Yeah, well, we haven't done anything the usual way, so why start now?"

Brady moves his hand to my thigh. "As long as it ends up with you naked I'm all for it."

It's been over three months since I gave birth to our

triplets, and now that they're weaned I am getting slices of time back. Even though we signed an alliance with the Robichaux months ago, tonight is the official celebration of our union. We're having dinner with the new leadership council of eight. Donna and Annie join us for our side while Marion, Richard, and my siblings, Luke and Lucy, represent the Robichaux.

We've reached a metal gate that has a guardhouse. "Wow. Why don't we have one of these?"

Brady's voice deepens to almost alpha level. "We don't need it. Nobody dares to threaten us."

The memory of Sierra receiving an engraved baby rattle on her wedding day says otherwise, but I don't mention it as the car window lowers with a faint hum so Brady can speak to the guard. The uniformed man says, "Mr. Le Roux. Welcome. Let me buzz you in."

"Thank you."

We drive past tennis courts followed by a pond that has a small cottage beside it. As we turn the corner I'm awestruck by the sheer size of the mansion before us. It's an older home like many in this town, and while the putting green we just passed adds to the regal air, it's not as pretentious as I would have guessed. I smile at the porch swing and rocking chairs set by the entrance.

We've arrived before Donna and Annie. Brady turns the key to stop the engine and turns to me. "Ready to meet Luke and Lucy?"

Growing up, I had always wanted siblings, and when I heard about having two younger ones I entertained the idea we might have fun together. Lucy squashed that dream when she came to my tattoo parlor a couple weeks ago and called me a bitch.

I nod. I suppose I should be a little nervous, because they can't be thrilled I've taken away any hope either might have had for being alpha of the Robichaux clan. But I'm not. Their reaction to me will be trivial compared to the events I've experienced these last few months. "I've always wanted to be the bossy older sister."

An icy breeze blows at us as we make our way to the entrance. A tall stately man opens the door, but his cool persona is warmed by the smile he gives me. "Right this way. Your mother is in the sitting room." He leads us down a hallway of darkly stained wood, and I notice oil paintings on the walls that are full of light even though they appear to be quite old.

Marion is in the doorway, and we exchange air kisses. "I'm so happy to see you. I've been looking forward to this evening."

Brady hands her a bottle of champagne. "We have too. This is chilled, but don't feel as if you have to open it."

Richard's feet thump over a hardwood floor toward us. "I do have a few bottles ready." His smile seems genuine as he takes the bottle from Marion and inspects it. "But one never knows." He winks at me before leaning close to kiss my cheek. "I hope you're drinking again. This is a night for celebrating."

Marion says, "Right this way." She leads us past what

appears to be a parlor and into a room that is larger and decorated in shades of burgundy and brown. A fire crackles, but the young man leaning against the wall with his arms crossed is what captures my attention. His face breaks into a smile, and he stands tall when introduced.

"Brady, Carly, this is Luke."

Luke extends his hand to Brady in a fluid motion that makes me think he's quite practiced at social graces.

"It's a pleasure to meet you, sir." Luke's dark blond hair is neatly combed, and his Oxford shirt is starched to perfection.

Brady says, "Likewise."

I extend my hand to my brother, and he lifts it to his lips. "My dear sister."

He kisses me and then gives me a smirk as I mimic his tone. "My dear brother. It's nice to finally meet you."

Marion sweeps her arm to the side of the room where Lucy is standing. Her dress is quite short but fits her curvy body in an attractive way that would make Sierra proud. "And this is Lucy."

My sister makes no move to come closer and merely nods at us. I grin broadly as Brady says, "Lucy, what a pleasure."

She gives him a strained smile as I say, "Yes, it's nice to see you again. You look lovely tonight. What a beautiful dress."

Her eyes widen a touch before she offers a saccharine reply. "Thank you."

Ice rattles in a bucket as Richard removes a bottle of

champagne. "It's time for a drink. Lucy, bring me the glasses, please."

Brady says, "Luke, you must be getting excited for winter. It's supposed to be a cold one and great for skiing. You race, right?"

"I do. Dry-land training already started, and we should be able to get out on the snow next week."

Brady turns to me. "There is a ski area on the other side of this mountain."

"Really?"

Richard answers for him, "Yes. I bet you didn't know you came from a ski family. Your great-grandfather created it." His voice has a note of disdain, but when I glance at his face his smile reaches his eyes, and I shake off my suspicion.

Luke hands me a glass of champagne and says, "I'm sure there's a lot you don't know about us."

The glass is cool in my hand. "I'm sure there is. You'll have to catch me up."

Lucy snorts and then starts to cough when we all glance at her. She shakes her head and lifts her glass. "Sorry, went down the wrong way."

Luke asks, "Do you ski, Carly?"

"No, there's not a lot of that in Venice Beach."

He offers me a smile that suggests he is open to getting to know me.

"So tell me about school. What is your major?" I ask him.

"Engineering."

Having done a little research on the University of Maine at Orono, I learned that's one of the school's more competitive programs. "Good for you. I know that's a tough one to get into."

Luke nods and lifts his glass to me. "It is. But we Robichaux are a cut above the rest, aren't we?"

I smile back at him because he is making an effort to get along. I raise my glass too. "You certainly are. Ian was impressed with your fighting skills, and I've heard you're a good racer. With that kind of drive and determination I'm sure you'll be a great council member."

Richard leaves the room when the rumble of Annie's car sounds outside. I turn to Lucy to see if perhaps we can try too. "And what's your major, Lucy?"

"I'm undecided."

And I'm not surprised. Annie told me she's a party girl, and I think she plans to live off her inheritance rather than get a job. "I'm sure you'll figure it out. There's plenty of time."

She shrugs as Donna and Annie make their entrance. Introductions are made, and Richard hands them glasses of champagne.

Marion says, "I think it's time for a toast." She glances around slowly to command everyone's attention. "To a long and prosperous relationship that forges peace for the entire Northeast Kingdom."

Glasses clink and tart flavor floats over my tongue as we all take a sip of our drinks. Luke and I lock gazes for a moment, and he tilts his head toward me. But when I glance at Lucy she avoids looking into my eyes.

I return my attention to Luke. Maybe I'll get a sibling out of this deal after all. My sister can hate me all she wants; I'm well versed in mean girl, and I'm not threatened. I'd rather concentrate on my brother, because he's someone I want on my side. "Tell me Luke, what did you think when you found out I existed?"

His eyebrows rise, but he doesn't skip a beat. "I wondered what other skeletons we might have hiding in our closets." He takes a sip of his champagne while staring at me. He holds it in his mouth for a moment and then swallows before he asks, "What did you think when you found out about us?"

I glance at Marion and recall my shock when I discovered she was my mother. I find my pain over her abandonment has faded. I return my gaze to Luke. "I thought things were about to get interesting."

CHAPTER 3

Lily

THE FULL SKIRT of my dress rustles as I make my way to the kitchen. I look down at the shimmery gold chiffon layered over the sapphire blue silk. This gown is beautiful, and I felt like a princess when I first put it on. Right now I feel like Cinderella who's about to have her dress torn to shreds by the ugly stepsisters, because in a half hour all the important people of the Veilleux clan are due to arrive to meet me.

My insides roll with nerves, and I hope Carol has something to help with that. Her warm smile wraps around me like a hug as she says, "Goodness, you're stunning, Ms. Lily."

"Thank you. But I'm also a nervous wreck. Any ideas on how to settle my stomach?"

She nods and turns to the cabinet. "They're going to love you. You're kind, warm, and extraordinarily beauti-ful." A glass clinks on the granite countertop as she sets it down.

"You're sweet." I step back to look in the dining

room, where the server is polishing crystal. Then I move close to Carol and whisper, "But I'm afraid they'll all hate me like Patricia does."

A spoon clinks as Carol mixes baking soda in a few ounces of water. "Hush." She winks at me and whispers back, "Nobody likes Patricia. They'll be thrilled you've taken her place." In a normal voice she says, "Here, drink this quickly, and you'll be good as new."

I swallow the salty mixture in a few gulps. "Thank you. Now I'm off to find my husband and cling to his arm."

Carol takes my cup and shakes her head. "You'll do no such thing. You're worthy of your new position. Don't forget that."

I smile at her. "And you might need a raise. Thank you, Carol."

"You're welcome. Now go dazzle Victor before the guests arrive."

I leave the kitchen with a calm belly and renewed courage. So much so that I stop in the doorway of Victor's study to pose in my dress.

Victor's gaze moves up and down my body as a slow smile covers his face. He licks his lips, and he comes toward me. "That dress is going to look even better on the floor. You're delicious."

He grabs me by the waist and dips me in a dramatic kiss that leaves me giggling. When I'm upright I say, "You sure know how to help with my nerves. Thank you."

Victor raises a finger and points to his ear, and then holds his arm out for me. "Come. The masses are here to meet their queen."

I inhale deeply and take his arm as air rushes back out. "I'm ready."

Carol was right. Many of the people I meet seem to be happy to have me as the new prima. And while nobody has said anything outright against Patricia, the implications are there with veiled praise for her previous reign.

Conversations hum as I look around the room. An old man has my husband's ear as he drones on about the late alpha, Victor's father. When the man's eyes start to glisten I step back to let him share the private moment with my mate. Scanning the crowd I catch Luke's eye, and he winks at me before he nods toward the hallway. I glance over to see an older couple enter the room. I paste on my prima face and wait as they approach.

I touch my husband's arm lightly and speak in his head. *"Victor, I think the Robichaux are here."*

He excuses himself from the gentleman and steps beside me to greet them. "Marion, Richard, I'd like you to meet my wife, Lily."

Richard takes my hand and leans in to kiss my cheek. "It's an honor to meet you, my dear."

Marion's startling blue eyes study me for a moment, and I can't help but think of Carly. She takes both of my hands, and we exchange air kisses. "How wonderful to meet you, Lily. I trust you're settling in as prima okay?"

"I am, thank you." Remembering a few of Patricia's

lunches on her calendar involved Marion I add, "And I hear you're a fan of the Cat's Meow. We'll have to meet for coffee soon."

"Oh, yes. They make the most wonderful quiche, and we do need to chat."

Richard clears his throat, and Marion gives her attention to Victor. "It's high time we had another prima meeting. I'm eager to get Lily up to speed on what we do."

Victor's voice is cold when he replies, "Yes, but do try to keep an open mind, won't you?" He smiles, but there's no warmth behind it. "Now that you've teamed up with the Le Roux I fear you've tipped the scales in your favor, and we may not have much say."

Marion replies icily. "And here I'm hoping that you'll want to join us in creating a peaceful council of the three clans to rule the Northeast Kingdom." She glances at Richard before returning her gaze to Victor. "Perhaps you're the one that should come to lunch?"

Wow, she just totally dissed me as not being capable of making decisions for the Veilleux clan. While it's true I won't do anything without Victor's say, my bear has become restless and I take a slow, deep breath to calm myself.

Victor's low growl sounds as he replies, "We have great respect for the Robichaux; it's the Le Roux that make things difficult." His voice lowers to a level that even bear ears have trouble hearing. "My father's death came more quickly than it should have, and I can't help but wonder why."

What? Did Victor just imply the Le Roux killed his father?

Marion says, "I trust you're looking into that." She glances at me. "Rest assured we'll support any actions that become necessary."

Tiny hairs on my body stand on end as I think about her words. The Le Roux are cold-blooded killers, and I almost fell into their clutches. I slip my arm around Victor's waist and lean into him. My savior.

Luke has joined us, and I welcome his friendly face. He leans in for a quick kiss. "Things look serious over here. Need a break?"

Richard says, "Luke. You've met the prima?"

"We go way back." He reaches for my empty glass. "You need another drink. Come." Luke takes my arm and says to Victor, "I'll bring her back after I've gotten her into a bit of trouble."

Victor grins at him as he hits his shoulder. "No shots."

"What? I would never dream of such a thing."

Luke leads me to the other side of the room. "My mother can be intense. Are you okay?"

While I'm dying to ask questions about what just happened, I don't think it's appropriate. "I'm fine. Clan politics are bound to be stressful at times."

Luke grabs two glasses of champagne from a server that has stopped beside us. "They can be." He hands me my drink and says, "The trick is to learn when you need a break. Victor's been doing this for years, and he's a master at the game." Luke's face shines with admiration for my husband. "You'll get used to it." He takes a sip.

Will I? I had no idea how diabolical the clan relationships were, and I definitely didn't know to what lengths the Le Roux would go to remain in power. "I'll remember that." I look past Luke toward Victor. He's holding Marion's arm and speaking softly to her as Richard listens.

Luke leans in close to get my attention. "I think we might need shots after all. C'mon." He grabs my hand and pulls me out of the room with a grin. I can't help but go along with his playful move.

"Where are we going?" Our feet thump lightly down the hall.

"To Victor's study. I know where he keeps the good stuff."

I laugh softly as he yanks me through the doorway, and the door clicks shut behind us. "I'm not sure this is such a good idea."

"Of course it is. Victor asked me to keep an eye on you in case he got involved in weighty conversation."

"Weighty?" I grin as Luke holds up a bottle.

"Tequila?"

"Sure." Two shot glasses thump on the wet bar, and amber liquid trickles in.

He hands me one and says, "I knew I liked you."

I smile at him because this is a welcome distraction. "Thanks for watching out for me." We both throw back the drink, and the alcohol burns its way down my throat. An involuntary shudder runs through my body at the taste. And I realize that being a prima involves way more than lunch.

CHAPTER 4

Carly

I'M NOT SURE how Marion did it, but this morning she contacted me to say we have a prima lunch today with Lily. I can only imagine the lies Victor has told Lily about the Le Roux, and I'm mentally bracing myself to remain calm and logical throughout the meeting. The subject of Sierra's kidnapping has to be raised, and it's not going to go well with Victor's new bride. My heart aches for Lily, because she's about to learn that evil lurks in her husband.

I've arrived early and am still in the car. The visor snaps down when I lower it to check my makeup in the mirror. I pull another wavy tendril of hair from my loose ponytail. The few around my face should help me appear friendly instead of powerful. I need my compassion to be apparent, because the truth is, I don't want to hurt Lily.

The smooth hum of the Veilleux town car draws my attention, and I glance at it pulling into the parking lot. I'm not surprised when a driver lets Lily out and follows her inside the Jefferson House, the historic mansion turned restaurant where clan business is often held. She has to feel threatened knowing the Robichaux and Le Roux now have an alliance.

As tempted as I am to wait for Marion, I know I should join Lily by myself. She needs to see I don't have a reason for a buffer and that she shouldn't either. Snow flurries swirl around me, and one tickles the end of my nose as I make my way across the gravel drive. It strikes me that it's an odd surface treatment considering the tiny rocks must be shoved into a pile when snow plows clear it after a storm.

When I enter I'm led to the second floor and greeted by a hostess. From her cool look I have no doubt she's a Veilleux, and I wonder why I haven't noticed this place seems to be run by the rival clan. Soft classical music is playing, and the buzz from the main restaurant is faint. Lily's driver is sitting on a chair just outside the door. I smile at him before I enter, and he nods in my direction with a straight face as if to say he'll be watching my every move.

Lily is standing by the window, gazing out at the expanse of lawn that will soon be covered in a blanket of white snow. She turns slowly toward me. "Carly."

She's beautiful as a werebear. Her cheekbones are more prominent, and she holds herself with a poise I don't remember. It's more than the regal-looking dress she's wearing, and I realize she was born to be a leader, because she's come into her own. "Lily, you look happy. Being prima suits you. Annie will be so pleased to know you're well."

Lily blinks but quickly pastes on her show face. "Please give her my best." She steps away from the bright window and into the warmth of the room. "How are your children?"

She's good at this. "They're a joy. One I'm sure you'll get to experience next year. I'm told Victor is your true mate."

Lily nods and can't hide the faint blush that comes from the rush of love one undergoes when speaking about their mate. "He is, and it's an amazing thing, isn't it?"

"Yes, it really is. We're pretty lucky to have been called."

Lily studies me for a moment. "I should thank you for my tattoo. While things didn't end up as the Le Roux planned, I'm quite happy with my destiny."

Is she actually willing to consider a peaceful relationship with me? Patricia must not be very influential. "That's all I ever wished for you. Annie too."

Lily's eyes squint a bit. "Right." She wanders over to the table and touches the silverware before glancing at me again. "So how do these lunches work? I didn't get an agenda. Is this a free-for-all?"

"We do usually have an agenda, but Marion and I thought today would be better spent as an informational meeting. We'll go over the things we have done in the past and answer any questions you may have."

Footsteps alert us before Marion appears in the

doorway. We both glance at her as Lily says, "I see."

"Lily, Carly." My mother comes to us and holds out her hands. I grab one and notice Lily has no hesitation doing the same, so I reach for her other hand. She's reluctant but takes mine as Marion says, "My, we're a lovely group of prima. Great things are going to come from us, I can tell."

"Yes, I think so," I say. There's an awkward moment of silence when Lily doesn't add anything. The aroma of garlic is strong, and I change the subject. "I think appetizers are on their way. Let's sit."

As we get settled a waiter arrives, and ice clinks in his pitcher as he pours water for us. Marion says, "Your prima reception was lovely, Lily. Richard and I had a wonderful time."

"So did your son." She grins, and I catch a glimpse of the young girl I met in Colorado. "He's trouble."

Lily knows Luke? Marion snaps her napkin out to place it in her lap. "He does have a bit of the devil in him, doesn't he?"

"Yes. I'm afraid he and Victor are dangerous together."

My brother is friends with Victor. Interesting. While I'm not surprised that the Le Roux were not invited to Lily's prima reception considering Sierra's kidnapping and our rescue that left a couple Veilleux dead, I am curious as to why this is the first I've heard about the family relationship between the Veilleux and Robichaux.

Marion gazes at me. "Your friend Sierra must be having her babies soon. When is she due?"

Damn. I'd forgotten how she likes to lay things out on the table right away. "Poor thing. She's been pregnant since June and she's about to burst. I wouldn't be surprised if it's this week."

The waiter sets plates of shrimp and tomato in a garlic butter sauce before us. Marion cuts a piece with a loud clash. "Lily, do you know about Sierra's kidnapping?"

"Kidnapping? No."

Marion lifts a piece of shrimp toward her mouth. "It all started at Carly's wedding. It seems Victor was quite attracted to Sierra and decided to bite her on the dance floor."

Lily frowns and sets her fork down. Marion continues. "Now, this was before Victor met you, because he never would have gone for Sierra if he'd met his true mate. But..." She slides the bit of shrimp off her fork and chews.

Poor Lily is struggling with her emotions and is doing a bad job of hiding it. Marion swallows and says, "I'm not certain he knew that a bite to a half would change her. But he did know that it would create a mate bond that Sierra wouldn't be able to resist."

Lily shakes her head. "I don't understand. Why would he want to do that?"

Marion nods. "It confuses me too. Victor is an attractive man that could have his pick of women, yet he went after Sierra. Who was already mated to another man. That's frowned upon in our world." She shrugs and glances at me. "Carly? Can you provide some insight?"

"I only know Sierra's side. For weeks after he changed her, Victor spoke in her head about his feelings. He wanted to be with her, but Sierra was in love with Keith."

Lily leans forward and hisses at me. "No. You're lying."

Marion reaches over and touches her arm. "I'm afraid she's not. Victor kidnapped her and Carly to get what he wanted."

Dishes rattle on the table when Lily bolts to her feet. "Stop this! You two are not going to turn me against Victor."

The Veilleux driver has come into the room. "Ms. Lily?"

"I'm fine." She turns to us. "This meeting is over."

Marion speaks in a harsh voice. "Not so fast. You might also want to know that Sierra was rescued on the Fourth of July, since you married him just a few days later."

All color has drained from Lily's face, and she shakes her head before stomping out of the room with her driver by her side.

"Well, you certainly get the job done, Marion." I say.

"I wasn't willing to sit and pretend through an entire meal." She stabs a piece of tomato with her fork and juice oozes out. "It ruins my appetite."

CHAPTER 5

Carly

"*CARLY! COME QUICK.*" Ian's voice rings in my head, and the spray bottle I was holding thumps on the floor when I drop it to race over to Kick It. When I get there I find Luke setting an unconscious Taylor down on the couch.

"What happened?" I drop to my knees by her side.

Luke says, "I was on my way here, and she collapsed on the sidewalk. I caught her before she hit the ground. I think she fainted."

I stroke her heated face and speak in her mind. *"Taylor, can you hear me?"*

Taylor moans, and her eyes flicker. Ian says, "Thank God. Taylor, are you okay?"

She tries to sit up, but Luke pushes her shoulders back down. "Not so fast. You just fainted and need to give yourself a minute."

"Yeah. I remember." Taylor closes her eyes again. "I'm not sure I can work today." She sits up abruptly. "I'm going to be sick." But the movement must have been too much, because she drops her head between her knees. "I think I need Keith to come get me."

I say, "That's a good idea." Her face is pale when she raises her head to look at me, and drops of moisture glisten on her forehead.

Sierra has come over to see what's happening and says, "Ian, go get her some juice." She looks over at Luke. "You." She points toward the water cooler. "Go wet a towel with cold water and bring it to me."

Luke's eyes widen in surprise at Sierra's order, but he recovers quickly and moves to do as she asks.

Sierra kneels down beside me and says to Taylor, "Let's get something in you to raise your glucose level. What did you eat today?"

Taylor takes the juice Ian hands her. "Not much." Leather creaks as she sits back on the couch. "I'm fine now. It's probably just my fever." She takes the towel Luke has handed to her. "I feel so stupid, guys. Really, I'm fine."

Sierra plops down next to her on the couch and says, "No, you're not. What did you eat?"

"I had some tea—my tea. I had a travel mug with me."

Luke says, "I'll go get it."

The door clicks shut, and Ian asks, "Tea? You're worried about that?"

"Yeah. It's a special blend Nina made for..."

"For what?" Ian's voice is stern.

Taylor looks at Sierra's belly and snaps back. "It's fertility tea, okay? I'm having trouble getting pregnant."

"Nina Hamlin?" Ian's voice has a hint of a growl in it.

Wait. How doesn't she know? Werebear have a mating season. "Taylor, we can only get pregnant from May to July. Didn't Keith tell you that?"

Her brow furrows. "No. But I haven't talked about this with him. I was—"

"Stupid."

"Ian!" Sierra scowls at him.

"Oh come on. Everyone knows Nina practices black magic. I mean, the shop is nicknamed Dark Elements."

Taylor says, "Obviously I didn't. And what's it to you anyway?"

Ian crosses his arms as Luke enters the gym. "It's probably why you're sick. I don't trust that woman."

Ian grabs the mug from Luke. "I'll take care of that."

"No." I reach for it. "I'll take it."

"Anyone want to tell me what's going on?" Luke asks.

"What do you know about Earth Elements and Nina?"

"Nina Hamlin was an odd girl that turned her weirdness into a decent business by pretending she's a witch." He shrugs. "Kind of smart if you ask me. The tourists and college kids love her."

"So she's not the real thing?" I clutch the travel mug tight.

"Nope. She's just human."

I communicate with Taylor. *"While that may be true, I'm going to hold on to your tea if you don't mind."*

"Sure."

Ian squints at me and says telepathically, *"We'll talk later."* He addresses Luke. "As you can see, your trainer is in no shape for you today, but I am." He sweeps his arm toward the gym. "Shall we?"

Luke nods and turns to me. "Nice to see you again, Carly. And Taylor, I hope you feel better."

"Thanks. And thanks for catching me. I'm sure you saved me a nasty bruise."

"No worries." Luke follows Ian as he strides over to the martial arts center.

Sierra says, "So they're training your brother, huh?"

"Uh-huh. Richard wants his warriors to work with Taylor, and Lucy and Luke are doing it first."

"Oh wow, Taylor. You have to train Lucy? She's a total bitch," Sierra says.

Taylor swallows a mouthful of juice and grins. "She's not so bad. I think it's hard living in Luke's shadow."

Sierra lets out a low sound of disbelief from the back of her throat, and I ask, "Keith's on his way?"

"He should be here any minute."

My best friend touches Taylor's arm. "Hey, you can talk to us, you know. This is all new for us too. We're in this together, okay?"

"Thanks." She licks her lips and sighs. "I can't believe I spent so much time stressing over getting pregnant when it wasn't possible." She turns toward Sierra. "I didn't say anything to you guys because I didn't want you to feel bad for me. You should be happy over your babies instead of worrying about me."

"Then you need to spend more time with me. Worrying about other people is the thing I do best." Sierra hugs her. "Seriously. Let us help you do this whole werebear thing. Okay?"

"Okay." Taylor glances over at me and speaks softly. "Do you think the tea might be why I fainted?"

Warning bells are going off, and while I can't explain how I know, I'm positive it is dangerous. "I'm not sure. But I'll let you know what I find."

Taylor nods as the rumble of Keith's Jeep sounds in the distance. I send a message to my mother-in-law. If anyone knows about magic, it's Donna. *"Free for dinner? I need some information about witches and fertility tea."*

"I'll be over sooner than that for my baby fix."

Donna's words make me grin. She loves being a grandmother. But my smile fades when I notice Taylor holding her head. I send a message to Dr. Reynolds telling him I'm sending her his way. Then I talk to Keith before he comes inside. *"Take your wife to the hospital. I'll let her explain everything to you, but she needs to be tested. I think she may have been poisoned."*

I glance down to notice I've managed to dent the metal travel mug with my squeezing. Sierra may be worried, but I'm angry. Someone is trying to keep the next Le Roux generation from happening, and my money's on Victor Veilleux.

I ARRIVE HOME to Donna singing to the babies. She has them lying on a big blanket and is tickling their feet as they squirm to her song. The sight makes me grin.

"Hey, I had no idea you were such an entertainer." The couch whooshes as I drop onto it.

Donna stands and sits in the overstuffed chair where she can face me. "I've got a great audience."

"We dropped the ball with Taylor. She didn't know that werebears have a mating season. Seems she was worried about not getting pregnant and took to drinking a fertility tea mixed up at Earth Elements. She fainted today, and I think it's because she's being poisoned."

Donna gets up to move a baby play gym over Connell, who craves constant interaction. Audrey lets out a squeal when one is placed over her too. Little Elliot has fallen asleep. "Hmm, Nina Hamlin runs that shop. She's a strange one but human and most certainly not one with witch powers. I can't imagine she'd get mixed up in werebear business."

"I dropped the tea off at the hospital lab for testing. But I bet good money it's toxic." I perch myself on the edge of the chair as my bear stirs inside of me. "How do you suppose it got that way?"

Donna gazes at me intently for a moment before speaking. "The Veilleux medicine man. While our Kimi only practices good, I don't trust others do."

I've never met the Le Roux medicine woman, but the vision of Catori, the old Native American woman I met in Colorado, comes to mind. "Tell me more about Kimi. I know she helped you send out the call to fertile women with werebear heritage." I glance down at my children and grin. "And a pretty powerful call it was."

Donna leans over and scoops up sleeping Elliot to cuddle. "Our relationship with the Abenaki Indians is centuries old. Each clan has a spiritual Native American to help us with situations that require the spirits. It's possible Victor employed theirs to keep us from producing more children."

I get up, and my feet thump on the floor when I begin to pace. I tick off my fingers one by one. "Lily is now a Veilleux, Sierra is pregnant with Victor's babies, Taylor was being poisoned." I stop and gaze at Donna. "What's he got planned for me?" When Victor kidnapped Sierra with her full sleeve of tattoos on her arms, he was convinced she was the woman in the prophecy, "The tattoo girl will bear the greatest gift."

But he has to know that it was me now that Ink It is open, and it's no secret that I'm a tattoo artist. Donna shakes her head. "I don't know." She hugs Elliot tightly to her chest. "But if he thinks he's getting a hand on my grandchildren, he's sadly mistaken."

Brady steps through the door with a growl. "He'll never get close enough. Poisoning Taylor is just one more nail in his coffin."

My husband's choice of words makes me cringe, because I'm afraid there will be more than one death to deal with before this is all done.

CHAPTER 6

Lily

R AGE IS FIGHTING to surface as I control my breathing while I pound down the staircase of the Jefferson House restaurant. My fangs have slipped out, and if I'm not careful I could shift in front of humans. Although Thomas would get me out before it happened, I'm tempted to let the transformation take place. Because I want to turn around and claw out two sets of blue eyes.

How dare they! Victor wouldn't kidnap women. Cold air blasts me in the face when we step outside, and I notice the storm has arrived. Sierra must be insane. I already know the Le Roux lie, but Marion is in on this one. I thought she could be trusted.

"Ms. Lily, the car's right over here." Thomas leads the way, and I follow without a word. There has to be an explanation.

When we get outside I lift my face to the falling snow, and the flakes melt on my skin. *"Victor, I've just left a prima luncheon, and we need to talk."*

My mind flashes to earlier this morning. Victor made

love to me slowly, making sure he gave me multiple orgasms, and he left me with no doubt of his devotion before he went in to work late. Tears prick my eyes recalling the intensity of our bond.

"I'm on my way home, darling." He didn't know I was meeting with Marion and Carly today. He must suspect what they told me if he's coming home in the middle of the day. *Shit.* My stomach clenches at the thought of what I might find out.

Okay, so my husband was with Sierra before me. I can handle that. It's not like I'm a virgin or anything. But, why would he bite her? Is that some drunken werebear thing? The sensations that flood my body when I sink my teeth into Victor are an intense pleasure for both of us, and it's very personal. *No.* I can't believe he would bite her without consent. She had to have wanted it.

The windshield wipers beat steadily as slush splashes up from passing cars. I still can't believe Marion blind-sided me like that. I know it's almost impossible to cheat on your true mate, and I'm not concerned that Victor did. But kidnappings? That's just ridiculous. Hot tears fall from my eyes, and I turn my head as if I'm looking out the window so Thomas won't catch a glimpse of me crying in the mirror. How could I have been so foolish to believe that Marion would become a friend?

When we pull up the drive I see Victor's BMW already in front of our house. He must be concerned, because he doesn't usually park there. He steps out of his car when we pull up beside him to park. Before the engine is off my husband pulls my door open.

Holding out his hand he speaks in my head. *"Darling, I don't know what you're so upset about, but let me take away the pain. Come, and let's sort this out."*

As if a dam has broken, my crying becomes sobs, and Victor scoops me up into his arms. "Shhh, it's okay. I've got you now." I bury my face in his shirt, and the starched crispness is rough against my cheek as he brings me into the house and down the hall to his study.

The faint scent of smoke from a previous fire comforts me as he sets me down on the couch. Victor falls to his knees to place himself before me. He pulls a handkerchief from his suit coat and hands it to me. I wipe my eyes as the warmth of my mate's large hands stroke the edge of my thighs.

"Talk to me, Lily. What's wrong?"

"They told me about Sierra."

He sits back on his heels, and a muscle in his jaw jumps as his green eyes hold me in an intense gaze. "You know anything I had with that girl means absolutely nothing now that you're in my life, right?"

I nod as he stands. "I do. But I need to understand why they say you kidnapped her."

Victor has walked over to the wet bar, and glasses thump on it as he prepares to pour us both a whisky. "I met Sierra at Carly's wedding. She's quite attractive and set her sights on me."

I reach for the cut crystal Victor hands me. The oaky scent of the alcohol wafts up my nose and tickles when I take a sip. He continues. "I had been drinking and got carried away. On the dance floor we let our instincts take over, and the next thing I knew I let my passion get the best of me." Victor is standing before me and swirls the amber liquid in his glass. He smirks and says, "You know how I can be."

I can't help the small smile that forms on my face, and I nod in reply.

"I bit her. And she immediately began to change. I had no idea that would happen." He takes a long sip of his drink, and I recall the pain that came immediately after Victor bit me on our wedding night. "After that we had the ability to speak in each other's head and formed a mate bond. You know the undeniable attraction such a connection creates."

I do, and the thought of Victor with Sierra makes jealousy surge in my veins as I nod for him to go on.

"Once she was changed she began to flirt with me telepathically." He turns up a palm. "I flirted back but never expected her to come to me. She was with the Le Roux."

Come to him? The idea of what they did when she arrived makes my blood move past simmering to a boil. "They told me you were with her right up until a few days before we married."

Victor shakes his head and begins to pace. "It's not quite what you think." He stops by the fireplace and turns to me. "I tried to break things off with her after I met you. The moment I saw you for the first time, all feelings for

Sierra vanished. But she couldn't let go and wouldn't leave." He downs the rest of his drink. "She bit me, and because you and I hadn't been together sexually she strengthened our mate bond."

Now my rage had turned to nausea. Did Victor sleep with Sierra after he met me? I shake my head and hold up my hand to stop him from saying what I fear. He moves toward me and gets down on his knees at my feet. Moisture pools in his eyes, and he whispers, "I was weak and couldn't fight it, Lily. God, I hated myself for being with her, but it was as if she had me trapped as a sex slave."

A tear rolls down his cheek, and I reach out to wipe it away. I've heard that freshly changed teenagers some- times get into trouble when one bites the other and creates an attraction that can't be controlled. My poor husband had to have been so tortured. "How did you get rid of her?"

"I begged the Le Roux to come get the—Sierra. But she didn't go willingly." He reaches for my hand. "Lily, she said she was pregnant with my babies." My mate closes his eyes and takes a labored breath before he says, "I think she might be right."

No! I recall hearing the first litter born to a prime contains the next alpha. "She might be carrying the next Veilleux alpha?"

"If she's is indeed pregnant with my children, she is."

That bitch. She forced my husband to impregnate her with the next Veilleux clan leader. Did she want to be prima? I squeeze Victor's hand. I can't let her have an ounce of control over my mate. "If she is, those children belong with us."

"What? Oh, darling, what are you saying?"

Determination sets in as I realize that the Le Roux can't raise the next Veilleux prime or prima. I take my husband's face in my hands, and his skin is smooth under my palms. "I'm saying we get a paternity test to determine if we're about to become parents."

Victor's shocked look softens, and he takes both of my hands from his cheeks with a firm grip as he stands to pull me up. "You are amazing, Mrs. Veilleux. Would you really want to raise my children from another woman for the good of this clan?"

"Of course. Those Le Roux have no business with the heir to our clan." I shudder imagining the evil Victor's offspring would be subjected to. "They belong here."

Victor gazes down at me, and silver flickers in his eyes. "You are more than worthy of being prima and standing by my side." His voice is hesitant. "I'm afraid I may not be worthy of you, though. Can you forgive me for my weaknesses?"

The vision of Sierra kissing Victor flashes in my mind, but I push it out. "There's nothing to forgive. You're mine now, and that's all that matters."

Victor lifts my chin with a finger and whispers, "I am all yours, now and forever."

He crushes me with a kiss that reaches deeply into me, and I return it with the resolve of doing the right thing. For us and for the clan.

CHAPTER 7

Carly

I'M ANSWERING EMAILS and looking for any excuse to stop when the door to Ink It opens, and a cold breeze washes over me. I glance up and discover it's Lucy, and I smile to myself thinking how fitting that is. Although it's odd that she came in for her workout through my shop instead of using Kick It's door. "Hi, Lucy."

She wanders over to stand by the red leather couch that is set up by a small table with loose-leaf binders of tattoos for customers to look through. Lucy picks one up and starts to thumb through it before she speaks. "So, did you draw all of these?"

"Some. But there's two books with my father's designs and one of Sierra's." The green spine of the album she's holding indicates it's my work. "You're looking at mine right now."

Lucy snaps it shut and lowers it. The book thumps as she drops it from a couple inches above the pile. "I'm late." She strolls over to Kick It.

Sierra has just finished with a client and walks out of

her room just as Lucy passes. My friend raises her eyebrows as she gazes at me. I raise mine back and address her customer. "Great to see you again, Jules. Are you set up for your next appointment?"

"All set." The petite brunette glances back at Sierra before leaving. "Thanks."

Sierra waves at her. "You're welcome. See you in a couple weeks." Once the girl is gone Sierra says, "Hey, did you know Lucy draws?"

"No."

Sierra sighs as she lowers herself to the couch. Her belly is huge, and she's got to be uncomfortable. "Yeah, she told me last week. I said she should bring her sketches by for you to see, but I think she's nervous."

I come out from behind the counter and sit on the chair across from her. The wood is hard under my thighs. "Huh. I'm not exactly scary."

"True, but you are her long-lost sister that blew into town to become a big deal." Sierra lifts her feet up on the sofa and sprawls out.

I snort. "You look like the big deal right now."

She rubs her belly, "I know, right? I can't wait for these guys to be out of me."

"I hope they come before Thanksgiving next week. Donna will be giddy to have six babies to hold."

"Annie too. I hope you don't mind sharing your babysitters with me."

"Not at all. I'm looking forward to a big family dinner. I've never done the Hallmark movie version of

Thanksgiving." Growing up with just a father meant a small meal that eventually became going out for Mexican instead.

"Me too. My mom tried, but her heart wasn't in it, and we ended up going to turkey buffets." Sierra shudders. "Think about all those people touching my food before it hit my plate."

I chuckle. "I thought I was the germaphobe. Thanks, now you've ruined all-you-can-eat brunch for me for life."

Brady's voice comes through our internal connection. *"Just talked to the lab. Taylor's tea had lead in it."*

I hold up my hand in a stop sign to Sierra so she knows I'm communicating with Brady. *"Whoa, lead poisoning makes you crazy over time, doesn't it?"*

"It sure does. Want to go chat with Nina for me?"

"Will do. I'll keep you posted."

I stand to go get my jacket. "I need to go to Earth Elements and figure out how lead got in Taylor's tea."

"Lead? Wow, that can't be good."

"It's not." Nylon swishes as I slide my arm into my puffy coat designed to keep me warm in sub-zero temperatures. "I'll be back." I push against the wind with the door and leave.

Earth Elements is only a block down from Ink It. My feet crackle against the ice and frozen bits of snow on the concrete sidewalk, and the cold manages to make my ears hurt by the time I get there. A spicy scent I can't quite place greets me when I enter.

A voice calls out. "I'll be right out to help you!"

The shop is dimly lit and tightly organized with hundreds of items from floor to ceiling. I wander over to the tea display to investigate the brand names, but find it's loose-leaf tea in clear plastic dispensers with the Earth Elements labeling. Various-sized empty tins are on a shelf with a display of packaged ones next to it. I search for the fertility blend and can't find it.

I turn to the girl I heard earlier as she says, "Our teas are blended on the premises, and I can make a custom one designed for your specific needs."

I gaze at the tiny girl with jet-black hair and porcelain skin. She'd be more attractive if she weren't wearing dark eyeliner that gives her a half-dead appearance. "How does that work?"

"I've studied herbs and know what different plants can do." She tilts her chin at me and adds, "And I've been known to practice a little magic to help things along."

I shake my head slightly. "Don't. I'm not a tourist, and we both know you're not a witch."

The girl's brown eyes widen. "I—" She huffs and furrows her brow. "No, but I have access to someone just as powerful, and he helps me out."

Now we're talking. I smile. "That's exactly what I need to know more about. Who is it that helps you?"

"Tokala, a medicine man. He puts secret ingredients in them. He calls on the spirits and spells the blends for special things."

"Like fertility?"

"Yeah." Nina bites her lip and steps back so she can move behind the counter.

"You need to stop using him. The tea you've been selling Taylor has lead in it."

Concern floods her face. "Oh my God. Is she okay?"

The aroma I smell comes to me. It's a mix of ginger and turmeric. "She is now, but she was slowly being poisoned."

Nina wrings her hands. "I had no idea. Oh my God, I'll refund the whole thing. I'll—"

I touch her tiny arm and tower over her for effect. "It's okay. I know you weren't responsible. But if you continue to use Tokala, you will have to answer to me. Do you understand?"

She nods quickly, and I ask. "What's that smell?"

"My Thanksgiving tea." Her words almost mesh together as she speaks quickly. "It's not spelled or anything, just a mix of herb and spices I put together."

"I'll bet it's lovely. I'll take some."

Nina rushes out from behind the counter and knocks over a display of bracelets. "Oh. Um." She picks it up and metal chains jingle as she pushes the pile of fallen jewelry aside. "I'll deal with that later." Her hand darts out to the pre-packed tins of tea, and she grabs a large one to give to me. "Here. It's on the house."

"Thank you." The container is smooth in my hand, and I tuck it into my pocket. I lean against the door to push it open and smile at her. "You enjoy your Thanksgiving."

Nina pushes a strand of hair behind her ear. "You too. And tell Taylor I'm so sorry."

"I will. Goodbye, Nina."

My walk back to work is not nearly as chilly with the wind at my back, and I send a message to Donna. *"Does the name Tokala sound familiar? That's who made the tea for Taylor."*

A gust of wind makes snow from a rooftop spray in my face when Donna answers. *"It sure does. That's the Veilleux's medicine man."*

CHAPTER 8

Sierra

THE WARMTH OF hot water is relaxing my tight shoulders. The shower door clicks open, and I turn to Ashton stepping in with me. "I'm not sure there's enough room. My belly is the size of another person."

My naked and aroused mate presses against my back as his hands hold my stomach. "I can't help it. I have a thing about you and showers."

I lean back against him. "Are you here to claim me all over again?" The memory of sex in the bathroom at Victor's comes to me, and more of me gets wet. When Ashton came to rescue me, neither of us expected to find we were true mates and that we would seal our bond with a quickie before he got me out of the Veilleux clutches.

His tongue is rough against my skin as he licks water from my back. "Um-hmm."

"I've heard that sex can make contractions start. So let's do this."

Ashton's body trembles with laughter behind me. "Like you needed that for a reason." He reaches between my legs and slides a finger in me. "Always ready for me, aren't you?"

The truth is I am. I have the sex drive of a teenaged boy, and just thinking about my man can get me hot. I moan as my husband strokes me toward climax. The tile wall is cool under my palms as I brace myself and arch my back to allow him better access. Within moments I'm shattering with an orgasm.

My knees are weak when I turn to face Ashton. He kisses me, and water runs over my head when he pushes me back so we're both under the spray. I break away laughing.

His voice is husky when he says, "I think we need to take this to the bed."

I nod and move to the side as the handle squeaks while Ash turns off the shower. Only one position is comfortable for sex now, and I want a mattress under my hands and knees. I wrap myself in thick cotton to dry off.

Ashton rubs himself quickly and discards his towel on the floor as he opens the cabinet over the sink. He grabs a bottle of amber liquid, and I grin when the scent of vanilla and spice wafts toward me, because I'm in for a treat.

I climb on the bed and let my towel fall to my waist as I sit. Ashton's hands swish as he warms up the oil. Placing himself behind me, his legs stretch out to surround mine as he begins to squeeze my shoulders. I relax into it. "This feels amazing."

His massage moves down my back and he kisses my

neck. I sigh as he reaches around to fondle my breasts. They're incredibly sensitive with my pregnancy, and the slightest tweak of my nipples sends a jolt of pleasure through me. I lean my head back to kiss his mouth. Ashton's cock is hard against my lower back, and I crave him inside me.

I pull away. "Take me." I position myself on all fours for his entry.

After months of being together he still manages to stretch me wide as he thrusts into me slowly. "Sierra." Ashton lets out a guttural sound as he begins to pump. His oily hands grip my hips, and I rock with him to increase my pleasure. I wish he'd be more rough, but I know his gentleness is for the babies. I don't bother to tell him it's okay and let him care for us in his way.

Besides, I don't need it hard to come. When Ash reaches around to slide his slick fingers over my folds I begin to lose control and buck back for him to settle deeper. Waves of pleasure take me over the edge, and I do my best to hang on for my mate's climax. When the sweet heat of his release explodes in me I let go too.

When we finish we collapse in a tangled heap. I marvel at the size of my husband's arm and trace along the outlines of a muscle. "I never knew I could love someone as much as I love you."

"Same."

"Carly says I'll love our children more, but I can't imagine it."

Ashton twirls a strand of my hair. "I don't think it

will be more, just different. But one thing is for sure. I'm going to want to protect them as much as I want to protect you."

I lift up on an elbow to gaze into my husband's blue eyes. They appear steel gray. "And nobody could ever be safer."

I WAKE WITH the sensation that something isn't right. I'm not afraid, but my senses are on alert as if I'm being warned. Of course needing to pee so badly I'm about to wet the bed might be the reason why. Cuddled next to Ashton I'm warm, and the odor of massage oil and his musk makes me want to stay. But nature calls, and I get up to use the bathroom.

As my feet land softly on the plush carpet of our bedroom my stomach clenches. It isn't excruciating pain, but I think I'm having a contraction, and I wait for it to pass before moving. Once I'm done relieving my bladder I make my way to the window that has a view of the woodlands behind our house. The moon has cast an eerie glow, and I wrap my arms around myself as I imagine the evils that lurk out there.

I haven't gone to Fishing Gorge since Carly and I were kidnapped there, and I wonder if I ever will. Sadness settles in my heart at how a simple pleasure was ruined for the two of us the day we were taken. Another contraction hits, and I breathe deeply. *"Darling children of mine, I'm eager to hold you in my arms and share you with the man you'll know as your father."*

I turn toward the bed and speak softly, "Ash, honey, it's time."

I SCREAM WITH another contraction. I can't imagine how my stomach muscles can keep this up, because I'm exhausted, yet they keep on squeezing with all their might. The doctor gave me something to speed things along because I've been in labor for more than twenty-four hours. But it's not working. The babies don't seem to want to come out. Once the pain subsides I whimper, "I can't do this."

Ashton's face is close to mine, and the stale mint scent of his breath pisses me off when he says, "Yes, you can." He takes my hand. "It won't be much longer."

"You've been fucking saying that forever, Ash. I'm seriou—shit!" A contraction hits, and the pain makes my vision blur. I pant and give my husband the evil eye when he opens his mouth to praise me. "Don't fucking say it."

My husband nods, and when I'm done he speaks to the nurse. "Go get the doctor. She can't keep doing this."

Finally. Someone needs to get my evil spawn out of me before I slice my belly open myself. Dr. Caldwell pats my knee. She grins at me. "Spread 'em."

I used to find her banter amusing, but right now I'm in no mood. I lie back and widen my legs for her exam. A rubber glove snaps against skin as she puts it on. At this point having a hand shoved inside me is trivial, and I barely notice the invasion.

"Still not enough. We need to talk about other options."

"Do it. Cut them out." Muscles start to squeeze my belly, and I mutter, "I don't care." I swore I wanted a natural childbirth. Having gone through the change, I thought I could handle normal pain. But I didn't expect this to go on forever, and right now I want drugs.

Ashton says, "Do it."

The wheels of my bed rumble down the hall as my labor nurse explains what's going to happen. All I get out of her words is that my agony will soon be over, and I'll wake up with three babies in the world.

Six hours later, I do. My husband says, "Babe, you did it."

I blink my eyes to shake off the feeling of not being quite real. "Where are they?"

"I just pushed the call button. I'm sure the nurse will bring them right in for you." Ashton sweeps my hair out of my face. "They're beautiful." His eyes shine with moisture, and the desire to cry makes my throat thicken.

"Have you decided the names?"

"Of course not, we need to do that together. Are you still happy with Jackson, Jason, and Justin?"

"Yes. Oh my God, how are we going to tell them apart?"

Ashton chuckles. "You'll know."

"Yeah, I may need sticky notes for the first few days."

The tiny cries of infants approach, and two nurses

walk into my room. The matronly one says, "You've got some hungry boys here. Time to feed them."

The younger nurse brings one to me and shows me how to get him to latch on. When he does, a toe-curling contraction makes me wince. The nurse says, "That pain you feel is normal. Your body is trying to shrink your uterus back to its regular size."

I gaze down at my son, and tears fill my eyes. He's the most beautiful thing I've ever seen, and Carly was right: my heart is about to burst with the love I feel. I glance up at Ashton holding another one of our children. Hot moisture rolls down my cheek. "They're perfect."

Ash smiles down at me. "They are. We're a family now."

I reach up to hold his hand. "This is the best day of my life. I don't want it to ever end."

"It won't. Things are only going to get better. Promise."

A hint of fear passes through me as I wonder if that's really true, because Victor could change everything in a heartbeat once again. But I shake the thought and hand my sleepy baby to my husband to make way for the next one. I refuse to let evil ruin my joy.

CHAPTER 9

Carly

I'VE NEVER LOOKED forward to Thanksgiving Day, because it was practically a non-holiday for my dad and me. But this year I'm excited. Metal hangers scrape over the bar in my closet while I look for an outfit to wear. Back to my pre-baby body, I get to dress in something that makes me feel pretty again.

I come across the dress I borrowed from Sierra the night I met Brady. It feels like a lifetime ago that I discovered my true mate, even though it's been less than a year. I smile with the memory of kissing him under the stars while in the cupola on top of this house. I'm going to have to drag him up there later tonight and do it again.

Donna's voice carries up the stairs as she squeals over the babies. I envision her handing off food to Annie and scrambling to get out of her coat before scooping up a child to hold. She wasn't joking when she told me being a grandmother was one of her greatest wishes, because she would spend every day with them if she could.

I finally decide on a burgundy crushed-velvet dress

that is soft in my hands as I pull it over my head. I'm eager to see Sierra and her triplets. I'm sure she's exhausted only four days after having a C-section, but we couldn't miss spending part of this day together, and she insisted on coming. I told her we would go to her if she wanted, but Sierra looked at their first excursion as an adventure. As if my thoughts called them, Sierra and Ashton's new SUV rumbles up the drive, and I scurry to finish getting ready.

My feet tap quickly on the stairs as I jog down to get to their car to offer help. When I open the door I chuckle to myself, watching Ashton approach with a huge floral diaper bag over his shoulder and two car seats in his arms. "That's a good look for you, daddy."

He grins back, "It sure is."

I walk to a waiting Sierra and take the third baby's carrier from the car for her. Her cheeks are surprisingly rosy as she shuffles along, and I ask, "How are you feeling?"

"Unbelievably happy. Like I'm going to explode with rainbows, puppies, and unicorns."

There's no hint of sarcasm, and I link my arm in hers. "How about you eat too much Le Roux cooking instead? I'm told Brady's stuffing is legendary, and I'm going to go snitch some. Want a bite?"

"Of course. My God, I had no idea how hungry breastfeeding three kids would make me. I'm ravenous." She steps gingerly up the stairs to our house.

I offer support with my arm, and she leans heavily on

me. "Does it hurt?" I ask.

"A little, but it's not something I can't handle." She stops in the doorway to gather herself. "It smells delicious in here."

Annie rushes over to us. "Oh, goodness, let me have that baby. This one's Jackson, right?"

Sierra raises her eyebrows at me as she steps inside for me to shut the door. "Yes. How did you know?"

I nudge my friend. "She's the baby whisperer."

Annie shoots me a smile and coos to the little boy. "You are the sweetest thing. Come meet your new friends. I have a feeling you're going to be the trouble maker, putting frogs in your mother's tub like Brady did."

I grab Sierra's arms with my sudden joy. "Our children are going to grow up together. We're going to do play dates and tacky birthday parties and sit on hard bleachers to watch soccer games. How awesome is that?"

Sierra hugs me. "It's amazingly awesome."

I lead her past the array of babies Donna and Annie are tending to and into the kitchen with Brady and Ashton. Bottles clink as the men connect their beer bottles. Brady leans over and kisses Sierra on the cheek before taking her jacket. "So good to see you. Ash and I were just toasting your family."

"Thanks. Now where's that stuffing I heard about? I'm starving."

"Uh-uh. You don't get to taste it until dinner."

I roll my eyes and say, "Don't you guys have football to watch?"

"And children to care for?" says Sierra.

Ashton hits Brady on the shoulder and starts walking to the living room. "We just got our orders. C'mon."

My friend thuds down on a chair at the kitchen table. A cheese and fruit plate is on it, and she grabs some cheddar and puts it on a cracker as she sighs. "I'd kill for a margarita right now."

"How about juice?" The cabinet clicks open, and I choose a glass.

"That'll do, thanks." She gazes out the window while orange liquid splashes in the cup. "Annie's gardens look beautiful even under snow. That woman is so talented."

"I know. I'm grateful she's in my life." Brady's stuffing is on the counter waiting to be reheated when it's closer to dinnertime. The tinfoil crinkles when I peel back a corner.

"I wish she could have a family with Ian. They're so adorable together."

"Me too." Annie is part of the generation of Le Roux women who are infertile, and I sigh thinking about how sad it is she won't know the joy of motherhood. I wish she'd at least let herself be happy in love. "I keep hoping that she'd ask him to move in. But I think she tortures herself with the thought of Ian's true mate coming along to steal him away."

I hand Sierra an overloaded spoonful of the breaded filling and put my bite in my mouth. Savory flavor pleases my taste buds. "Oh, this is good, isn't it?"

Sierra just moans before she swallows. "Look at us.

We both have amazing lives and want to spread the love. We're pathetic new moms."

I smile at my best friend. "I wouldn't want it any other way."

She winks at me and waves her spoon to indicate she wants another bite. "Me either."

Annie walks into the kitchen and hugs Sierra's shoulders. "I love you guys so much for wanting me to be happy." She sits across from her and reaches toward the plate of appetizers. "But I've watched what happens when a true mate comes along to shatter a relationship. It's not pretty, and I don't think I could survive it."

Sierra nods, and I guess she's thinking about how she moved on from Keith so quickly when she met her true mate, Ashton. "It sucks you only get one true mate. Are you sure?"

My sister-in-law shrugs. "Before you two came along I thought I was sure about everything bear clan. But when Brady changed Carly and we found out a half could become a werebear, I learned nothing is absolute. Just because we haven't seen it happen doesn't mean it couldn't."

I join the girls at the table and take a grape as Sierra reaches for Annie's hand. "I'm going to wish on every shooting star for you to find another one."

I swallow the sour fruit in my mouth to speak. "Now that we have an alliance with the Robichaux we're bound to mingle more. Maybe one is out there for you, and it's only been because of the isolation of the clans that you've never met him."

Sierra says, "Yes! I'm going to hold on to the hope for you, Annie."

Annie smiles at us, but her lips don't quite turn up enough for it to be real. She stands and opens the oven. The delicious aromas of sage, thyme, and turkey make my stomach growl as she says, "I've got a meal to finish, and we'll be eating in about a half hour. Go get your babies squared away so you can enjoy it."

Thirty minutes later we're all seated at the dining room table while Brady makes a show of cutting the turkey. I shake my head at his theatrics as the zing of a knife sharpener sounds. Dishes clash as bowls full of food are passed around.

Ashton says, "It's a bird, not a lion, cut it already."

"One must always be prepared for the task. I'm not a half-ready kind of guy."

I glance at Donna, who's smiling at their interaction. I suspect she loves having a full table for the holiday this year. I smile at her when she catches my eye and speaks to me. *"Thank you for making him so happy."*

"Thank you for raising a wonderful man."

Ashton raises his wine glass, and berry-colored liquid sloshes around as he says, "To the Le Roux clan for continuing on." He gazes at Sierra across the table. "And to my beautiful wife. May our lives always be full of joy."

Sierra lifts her glass to take a sip and then says, "To my best friend Carly, for taking me on a crazy road trip to our destiny. And to my amazing husband, for loving and protecting me no matter what."

Annie and Donna both say something that involves the babies. Rich merlot flavor flows over my tongue when I drink again. "My toast is for Annie and Donna." They're sitting next to each other, and I tilt my glass toward them. "To the women who keep this family running and full of love. I'm grateful to have you in my life." The three of us touch our goblets first, and the ring of fine crystal seems to sing like the family connection we have.

Brady makes the final toast. "I know you all think I'm going to talk about the mighty Le Roux clan and our future, but I think something else needs to be said." He lifts his glass. "May our lives continue to be full of pleasant surprises, and may we have the wisdom to accept what we're given with grace and compassion."

I think about the many events that have happened in the past year and how my new life was all brought about by a dream. The skin on my wrist is smooth as I rub over my tattoo. Pleasant surprises. That is what this year has been about. I clink my glass with Brady and take a sip as I vow to lead the clan with poise and love. Because nobody knows better than I do how life can change in a matter of minutes.

After we gorge ourselves on Thanksgiving dinner Sierra leaves with Ashton to go home and meet his parents for pie. Brady and I have the same commitment with Marion and Richard. The aroma of coffee is in the air as Donna and Annie help me dress the children for the cold temperature. I expect they'll have a nice mother-daughter chat over dessert while we're gone.

Brady lifts two babies up in his arms, and I grin at the paisley diaper bag he has over his shoulder. "You and Ashton are rocking the dad look."

He flashes me a smile. "Get used to it. Mating season is only a few months away, and I expect to make this fashion statement for a few more years."

I chuckle and think maybe another set of triplets next year might not be so bad. And then I imagine trying to put six tiny children to bed at night. I raise my eyebrows at him. "We'll talk."

As we walk toward the car I notice a storm is on its way. The sky is overcast, and moisture hangs in the air. "Are we supposed to get snow tonight?"

"Uh-huh. A nor'easter's coming. We could get up to two feet."

"Nice." This California girl hasn't experienced her first blizzard, and I'm a little excited. Brady has opened the car door for me and gone to the other side. I reach in with Audrey's baby seat. It snaps into the base with a loud click. I gaze across the car at Brady. "Could today be any more perfect? I can't believe a year ago I was eating nachos at a bar full of people without families. And now look at me."

Brady leans across the children, and I move to meet him in a kiss. When he pulls away he tucks a loose strand of my hair behind my ear. "This is the first of many. I love you, Carly."

"I love you, Brady Le Roux."

CHAPTER 10

Taylor

AFTER A FEW days of rest, I'm feeling antsy with restless energy. I've managed to catch up on the laundry, and the dryer door slams when I shut it. I wander into the kitchen for something else to do. Once the doctor told me I had toxins in my system that were causing my symptoms, I was relieved to find I'm not going insane. A handy white pill twice a day is flushing out the poison so that my chronic headache is gone, my body no longer aches, and I'm eating normally again.

The shouts and squeak of sneakers rise above the drone of the announcer on the television. Keith must be watching the Celtics basketball game. Bright light shines when I open the refrigerator to get the strawberries I cut earlier and the whipped cream. My husband has been such a kind caregiver that I think he needs a proper thank you.

I glance down at my shirt and sweatpants. This won't do. I set the fruit down on the counter to return to the laundry room and change into a sexy bra and thong instead. The air is cool and goosebumps form on my skin, but they won't last long considering my plan.

On my way to the living room I grab dessert. The whipped cream can is cool in my hand, and the scent of fresh strawberries tantalizes my taste buds. Keith is engrossed in the game and doesn't notice me until I stand in front of him and bend over, letting my breasts practically fall out of my sexy-but-impractical bra to set the bowl of fruit on the coffee table. "Dessert?"

A smile turns up the corners of his mouth as he lifts the remote to click off the TV.

I pop off the top to the can and shake it. "I don't want to interrupt your game."

The remote thumps onto the couch where Keith tosses it. "They were losing anyway."

Keith lets out a low growl as I climb onto the small table between us and sit cross-legged, showing pretty much everything I've got except what's covered by a thin strip of material. I take the bowl and place it in my lap. Cream whooshes out of the container as I squirt some on my cleavage. "Hmmm, that's too bad."

My husband's eyes glimmer with lust, and I grab a piece of strawberry from the bowl to slide it through the cream. "Berry?"

Big hands grab my hips as Keith pulls me to the edge of the table, and he gets on his knees. He bites the berry in my hand and moves to my chest to lick the cream. I purr like a cat when his mouth moves to my breast to suckle my nipple, and he removes my bra.

He stops and grabs the whipped cream. "Lie down."

I pick up the strawberry bowl and put it on the floor before I lie flat on the coffee table. The smooth varnished wood is hard under my back, but the sensation is quickly replaced with the chill of sweet cream that Keith sprays in a line going down from my neck to the top of my panties. He gazes down at me and shakes his head as he tosses the can onto the couch. "I can't eat all of this by myself." A twinkle in his eye makes me giggle, and he pulls off his shirt.

I prop myself up on my elbows to watch as the zipper of his jeans grinds when he lowers it. "Oh, goodie, you're going to share."

Bones thud on the coffee table when Keith climbs over me in his naked glory. He smears the white foam between us as he presses against me with his chest and I giggle. "You're crazy."

"About you."

"This is kind of—" Keith kisses me, and I squirm under the slippery feeling.

When he breaks to yank my panties down he says, "Let's move to the couch. This table is hard."

I stand and grab his cock. "Um hmm, so's this." I lick his chest, and sweet dairy coats my tongue. Shoving him onto the couch, I kneel between his thighs and take him in my mouth.

He moans and bucks his hips up. "Your idea of dessert is perfect."

I suck and bob over him until he pushes my head

away. "God, I want to sink deep inside of you."

Keith pulls at my hips to taste me, but I straddle his lap and rub my sensitive folds against his dick. "That's where I want you too." My mate loves it when I take control, and I lower myself onto his large appendage that fills me completely. I try to move slowly, but the need for friction is great, and I pump hard.

My husband's fingers pinch my nipples, sending a mix of pleasure and pain to my core as I ride him and let myself go. Keith is naturally a sweet, gentle lover, but he's learning to act on my need for things to be rough. "Pull my hair."

My head snaps back when he yanks, and my mate sinks his teeth into my shoulder. I'm close to orgasm anyway, and the rush of ecstasy that comes from his bite pushes me over the edge. He groans as his release spurts inside of me. My pleasure is slow to fade when Keith rubs my clit as I cry out.

Coated in dairy and our juices, I begin to lift myself off Keith so he can go wash off.

His grip is strong on my hips as he tugs me back. "No." He shakes his head slowly and gyrates under me. "You take me places I didn't know I wanted to go. Be messy with me for a little longer."

I rake my sticky fingers through his hair. "You rebel."

"You make me want to break the rules."

I tug his head back with a growl and let my bear come to the surface as I lower my mouth to his chest. "I didn't know there were any." I plunge my fangs into sinewy muscle and relish his scream of passion.

I'M STANDING IN the bathroom looking at my nude body in the mirror. My belly is distended because I'm very pregnant. I rub my taut skin as I notice Keith step behind me. He's grinning when he says, "Just a few more days and their screaming will make us wish those babies were still inside you."

His strong hands massage my shoulders, and I close my eyes to revel in the relaxing pleasure. A laugh startles me, and I open my eyes to the familiar sound of the old Native American man that has been haunting me. He's replaced Keith behind me, but because he's shorter I step aside to see his reflection in the mirror. Bony fingers reach toward me as if he's going to grip a doorknob. The man pulls his hand back toward his body, and an odd sensation of something being sucked out of me makes me glance down at my stomach. It's shrinking in size-oh God! He's stealing my—

The old voice pierces my head like a knife. "Drink the tea, and they'll remain yours."

I turn to face the man and find he's holding three tiny babies in his hands. I open my mouth to scream—

I bolt up in bed and realize I'm in the dark bedroom I share with Keith. Sweat slicks my skin, and I try to push the sheets off me, but I'm tangled in the linens. Quietly, so I don't wake my husband, I disengage myself from the damp cotton. My mate is snoring softly, and I slip out of bed.

The wood floor below my feet is a welcome coolness as I pad my way down the hall toward the stairs. I'm too upset to try to sleep and need some time to process what just happened. I had hoped my odd visions of the old man would stop now that I haven't drunk the fertility tea in a couple of days. Right now I'm not so sure I was poisoned. It had to be something else, because the dream I just had was as real as the original call to come here last spring.

The yellow glow of a nightlight illuminates the kitchen, and I put the teakettle on the stove to boil. I recall the visions I had that brought me to Maine. If I hadn't followed my gut I wouldn't have met the love of my life.

The cabinet clicks open, and I rummage through my tea collection searching for chamomile. But that's not what I want. I need the fertility blend, because if I don't drink that tea I'm not going to get pregnant. I know this like I knew I needed to move here.

Where the hell is it? Keith threw it in the garbage over a week ago, but because of the holiday it must still be there. It's in the container we keep in the garage. I walk over to the mudroom off the kitchen and pull open the door that leads to our cars. The concrete is cold under my bare feet, but I don't take the time to put on shoes.

When I open the bin the unmistakable stench of rotting fish remains accosts me, but I'm not deterred, and I yank out the top bag to get to the one below. The plastic is slippery in my hands as I carefully untie the bag. Junk mail is coated in coffee grounds that are coarse against my fingers as I sort through waste. Below slimy lettuce I retrieve the tin full of tea. Relief washes over me as I retie the bag and toss the other one back on top.

I'm startled by Keith opening the door. "What are you doing out here?" His hair is standing up on end, and his voice is sexy with sleepiness.

Shit. "Nothing, babe. I was just searching for an earring I lost." I tuck the tin into the back of my pajama pants. "I didn't find it. I was just coming in."

Keith's brow is furrowed. "It couldn't wait until morning?"

"I couldn't sleep. I know it's silly, but I just had to come check." I don't want to walk by him so I stop before the door. The laundry room is just off to the left once we're inside, and I need to hide my tin. "My hands are gross, and I think I got stuff on my pants. I'm going to wash up and change."

"Sure." The kettle screams in the kitchen, and Keith moves toward it. Once he removes it he asks, "Want me to sit up with you?"

I call out from the laundry room. "No. No, I'm fine. Go back to bed. I'll be up soon."

His voice carries over the rush of water in the utility sink. "Okay. Love you."

"Love you, too." Once I'm sure he's climbing the stairs I slip the tea container out of my pants and rinse it off.

After I change my pants I return to the kitchen, and utensils rattle when I pull open a drawer to find the mesh steeping ball. The lid pops off the tea tin, and I scoop some up. I drop the tea into my mug with a clatter, and I'm interrupted by Keith. "Earring?"

I glance over at the kitchen table and wonder how I didn't notice him there. Anger surges in me. I should explain this to him. "I—"

The old man speaks in my mind. *"He won't understand. You know what you must do."* I shake my head as if I can make him go away.

Keith is walking toward me. "Hey." His voice is soft. "What's going on?"

Fear makes my pulse quicken when I realize he's going to stop me from drinking the tea. My muscles tense as his hands land lightly on my shoulders, and I snap. I apply a power slap that knocks Keith out cold.

His body thumps onto the ground, and I step back. I blink in confusion, but an undeniable purpose overcomes my thoughts. "Well that makes things easier."

Steam rises from my mug as I pour hot water into it. The steeping ball clinks against my cup as I swirl it, and I glance down at my unconscious husband. "We're going to have triplets and be so happy, babe. You'll see."

PART 2

CHAPTER 11

Taylor

TINY BITS OF broken glass shimmer in the brightly lit kitchen. The metal chandelier lies on the tile floor next to Keith, and I survey the scene to make sure it's believable. The old man who seems to reside in my brain laughs, and it sends an involuntary shiver down my spine. My mate groans, so I kneel down to stroke his cheek. "Baby, are you okay?"

He blinks in confusion before he reaches up to touch his forehead. He winces at the contact and whispers, "You hit me."

"What? No. You're confused. The light fell and hit you in the head."

"Taylor, I know what took place." He sits up and notices the shattered light bulbs on the floor. His brow furrows in confusion. "How did this happen?"

"I don't know. It was the craziest thing. We were talking about tea, and the next thing I know, the chandelier crashed down on to you."

"Right. The tea." Keith winces as he stands. "Where is

that tin? The one you dug out of the garbage."

Keith caught me digging through trash searching for tea that was supposedly poisoning me. But I know better. "I didn't dig any tea out of the garbage." I rise to my feet and put my hands on my hips. "I was searching for my lost earring."

"Oh really?" Keith snatches a container off the counter. "Then what's this?"

"Chamomile. Seriously, Keith, I know I was stupid to drink the fertility blend. And I'm really sorry that I didn't talk to you about it first. But give me a little credit. I'm not an idiot."

He sniffs the crushed leaves and shakes his head. "Oh."

I walk over to him with concern on my face. "Babe, you must have a concussion." I gaze back and forth between his eyes. They're normal, but I have to continue the ruse. "One pupil is larger than the other. Sit."

Keith slumps down in the kitchen chair and drops his elbows onto the table with a thud before he holds his head. "I'm sorry, babe. I don't know what's wrong with me. Maybe I dreamt it." He lifts his face to me and offers a weak smile. "Are you sure you didn't hit me?"

I grin at him. "If I did you'd be more than knocked out." I'm trained in Krav Maga, a street-fighting form of martial arts. I also happen to be the lead trainer for the Le Roux werebear clan warriors.

"That's true." He closes his eyes and lowers his head back into his hands.

"Let me get you some ibuprofen." I open the cabinet, and metal scrapes on wood as I place the unlabeled tin of tea back on the shelf behind one marked chamomile. It's full of the fertility blend I must keep drinking if I want to get pregnant next spring. I toss the bottle of aspirin to Keith before grabbing a cup. Water rushes into a glass as I hold it under the tap.

Bits of light bulb crunch under my boots as I walk across the kitchen to hand it to Keith. "You sit while I sweep up this mess. You didn't step on any of it, did you?"

"No. I'm fine." His brow is knit in concentration, and I'm afraid he's thinking about what really happened.

"You know, I never really liked that chandelier. It must have been fate that it fell." The old Native American man that is helping me fulfill my destiny to bear Le Roux children comes to mind. "Now we get to pick out one we both like."

"It's so strange that it broke."

Keith reaches for the metal fixture, and I fear he's going to inspect it. I grab it first. "I've got this. You sit tight before you cut yourself." While I tried to slice the wire in a way that it appears frayed, I'm not sure my husband won't figure out it's been tampered with.

"Taylor, give me that, please."

Damn it. I place the heavy metal on the table with a thud. "Do you think maybe it wasn't installed correctly?"

Keith shakes his head. "No. I hung it." He's rolling the cord around in his hand. "This looks like someone deliberately hacked away at it." His eyes are big when he glances up at me. "I think this was meant for you."

Whew. The Veilleux clan is the Le Rouxs' enemy, and my husband thinks Victor Veilleux is behind the poison they found in my tea. I widen my eyes back at him. I'm tempted to cover my mouth with my hand, but that's probably going too far, so I say, "Oh my God, do you think it's Victor?"

My mate nods. "I do." His fists clench, and his face indicates he's speaking telepathically. I assume it's Brady he's talking to and continue cleaning up the mess. Shards of glass clink when I sweep the pile into a dust pan.

Dawn's salmon-colored light shines outside, and I realize it's going to be a long day as I pretend I'm worried about Victor's evil. I'm also betting Keith won't let me return to work as planned. *Oh crap!* We have a morning breakfast meeting at the Le Roux house today, and I'm going to have to continue to lie. Great. Well, at least my worry will be real, because I can't get caught in my deception.

I glance over at my travel mug with my next dose of tea. "Hey, should I make some coffee since we're both up for the day?"

"That would be great. I'm going to go take a shower."

Keith leaves the room, and I listen for the water to run before I grab my mug of tea and guzzle it down. I shudder at the disgusting taste and move to the sink to rinse my cup. When I get there, a wave of dizziness makes me grab onto the cool granite countertop. I close my eyes, and a vision appears.

I'm in a park and walking behind a tall thin woman with her dark hair blowing in the breeze. As I get closer, I notice she's pushing a stroller, and I know it's carrying my children. I call out for her to wait. She must not hear me over the wind that is now howling. I begin to run, but she's still out of reach, and I push myself to go as fast as I can. It's no use; the lady manages to stay too far ahead for me to catch up. Despair sinks into me like the cold, and I fall to my knees with the pain of losing my babies.

Suddenly it's quiet, and only the slightest breeze blows. I lift my face to the voice of the Native American man I've been seeing in my visions. He stands right in front of me along with the woman and says, "You know what to do."

I focus my attention on the woman. Her face is older than I expected, but I know it well because I've carried it in my heart all my life. She fades away like a ghost, and a shiver runs through me.

Whoa. I shake my head and refocus on rinsing out my travel mug. The water from Keith's shower stops, and I realize I haven't started the coffee. I scurry to get the task done, and brown liquid begins to drip when my husband returns to the kitchen.

He tilts his head at the pot and frowns. "What were you doing?"

I smile and walk over to him. "Daydreaming." I point out the window at the yard. "I think a swing set over there would be nice. That way I can watch our kids play while I make dinner."

Keith comes to stand next to me with two steaming mugs of coffee. He hands me one, and it's hot against my palm. I wrap an arm around his waist, and the flannel of his shirt is soft on my cheek when I lean against his chest.

"You're really anxious to have a family, aren't you?"

A bird feeder is set up in the snow-covered garden, and I watch chickadees take their turn getting breakfast. "I am. I know it's what I'm here for, and I've never been patient when it comes to getting things done."

Keith kisses the top of my head. "I've noticed."

I step away from him and gaze into his eyes. "Aren't you excited, too?"

He waggles his eyebrows at me. "About getting you pregnant?"

I grin. "About our future. I know great things are going to happen. You'll see."

CHAPTER 12

Sierra

THE WEEKLY BREAKFAST meetings at the Le Roux house have changed dramatically now that six infants are in attendance. It takes longer to get business accomplished, and I suspect Donna doesn't appreciate the divided attention when she speaks. I won't be surprised when she suggests we consider babysitters.

My spoon clinks as I stir cream into my coffee. I'm nervous about what I'm about to propose. Ashton and I decided it's for the best to be proactive about Victor's paternity threat. I slide a bite of sugary waffle goodness into my mouth to find it tastes like sawdust. I glance at my husband, and he winks at me. I swallow down the lump of food, but before I can speak my mind, Donna clears her throat.

Annie is bouncing Audrey on her lap, and when she glimpses her mother's face, her movement stops. "We have something of grave concern to discuss," Donna says. "Victor has made another move on Taylor. This morning, a chandelier fell on Keith, and upon inspection, it's clear it was tampered with."

Annie asks, "Keith? Are you all right?"

He nods. "Yeah. I might have gotten a slight concussion, but I'm fine."

Taylor puts her hand on his arm as she says, "He most definitely got a concussion, but I'll make sure he takes it easy." Keith smiles at her, but something's off. I wonder if they had a fight over the situation.

"I already have a team checking out their house, and we'll get to the bottom of this," says Brady.

Carly says, "Taylor, I know you can protect yourself, but I would like some guards to monitor your home. The Veilleux had to have gotten in there at some point, and we would be fools to not ensure it can't happen again."

Taylor shoots a startled look at Keith, and he frowns at her in reply. She takes a deep breath and speaks. "I know you're right. As much as I hate losing my privacy, it needs to be done."

Donna says, "Good, it's settled." She lifts her teacup and turns to me. "I have more business to cover. But first, what do you have for us, Sierra?"

"How did you know I wanted to say something?"

She swallows her tea and says, "Oh please, you've been jiggling your foot since you sat down. Out with it."

I push my knife in a circle on the table as I muster up my courage to face the inevitable. "Ashton and I think we need to prepare ourselves for a custody battle with Victor. He made it quite clear when he gave me the baby rattle engraved with a V at our wedding, and now that the babies have been born, I expect he'll do something to get them."

Annie hands Audrey a spoon to grasp and says, "You do know we don't do things like humans, right? This is a matter the prime and prima usually decide."

I nod. "I know this is something that has never come up between clans because nobody ever gets divorced."

Donna says, "I wouldn't say never. I've seen it when a true mate comes along." Audrey begins to bang the spoon on the table, and Donna glances quickly at Annie. So she stands up to pace with the baby instead. "Custody is usually awarded to the injured party in the relationship because they aren't abandoning the family they had," says the older woman.

"And because if an interclan relationship becomes a marriage, the couple pledges their allegiance to one clan, and our current situation has probably never been an issue, right?" I ask.

"Correct."

"That's why Ash and I want us to figure out a plan, because I don't think Brady and Carly are going to be able to work things out with Victor."

Brady thumps his fist on the table, and plates rattle. He says, "As much as I hate to admit this, the Veilleux do have a claim on your children, because one of them is their next alpha."

The tiny seed of fear in my belly blossoms into panic. I don't want Victor anywhere near my children. "No!" I stand up, and my chair scrapes across the floor. "That man cannot touch my babies."

Carly gets up and comes to me. She takes hold of my arms. "Hey. We won't let him hurt your kids, okay?"

Donna pipes in. "Victor is a lot of things, but he isn't stupid. He's not going to harm a potential heir and alpha to his clan. Brady's right; he does have a claim to your children."

A wave of nausea passes through me. *Oh my God.* "Ash?" Victor's face flashes in my mind, and his teeth gleam in the memory.

I turn from Carly to my mate's strong arms, and he pulls me against his chest. He says, "We'll figure this out. I promise."

I breathe in the scent of my husband and let it calm me. Ashton does make me feel safe, and I know he won't let anything bad happen to our family.

"There may be something we can do," says Donna. "Give me a few days, and I'll let you know what I find out."

Carly asks, "Kimi?"

Kimi is our medicine woman and the one that set the call in motion to get fertile werebear descendants here.

"Yes. It's about time we utilized her against the Veilleux." She glares at Taylor. "It seems they have no trouble with that tactic, so why should we?"

Taylor flinches, and a flush rises to her cheeks. A strong warrior like her must be embarrassed that she was unknowingly drugged and made a victim. I reach over to her. "Hey. Any one of us would have done the same thing. Please don't blame yourself."

"Thanks." Her expression relaxes into a smile.

I'm not sure why, though, because as much as I'd like to think I can comfort with just words, I doubt it's true. Unease niggles at me, and I communicate with Carly. *"Does Taylor's behavior today seem strange to you?"*

"It's probably the lingering effects of the poison." Carly frowns for a second and then masks her concern with a serious voice as she asks Taylor, "How's the training with Luke and Lucy going?"

"Good. Ian told me Luke is quite skilled. Lucy will get there once she gets in shape."

I'm reminded of the drawings Lucy showed me a few weeks ago. She's got talent but not the confidence to believe in herself. If she doesn't share her portfolio with Carly soon, I might have to intervene. A smile creeps across my face as I recall how my best friend mentored me as a tattoo artist. I think it would be a great way for the sisters to bond.

Carly says, "See that she does. I don't want her to hide behind her brother on this."

While the alpha tone is present, I know my friend well enough that her words tell me she senses Lucy's low self-esteem, too. Yup, it's time to bring another female artist into the world of tattoos. Besides, that will give me a purpose other than worrying about my babies.

Donna clears her throat loudly to command attention. Once all eyes are on her, she says, "There's one more thing to tell you. Years ago, when we first discovered our inability to create a future generation, we contacted a clan in the Arctic for help." She takes a bite of bacon to draw out the announcement that is about to come. "They denied us at the time, but I just got word they're reconsidering. It seems they're having trouble of their own and want to make a deal." She takes a bite of eggs and scans the table full of people to make sure the weight of her words settles in.

Brady's jaw is working, and I think this might be news to him, too. When Carly places her hand on his arm, I'm sure of it. One glance at Donna tells me she's enjoying her moment of power, and if I didn't feel sorry for her now that she's usually the least important person in the room, I would make a snide remark. Instead I watch the drama unfold.

Annie jumps in to keep Brady from exploding. "I'm sure you plan to put them in contact with Brady and Carly now."

"Oh. Yes. That's why I'm telling you this morning. Tristan and Isabelle De Rozier should be here next week."

Brady clenches his fists and restrains himself as he thumps the table instead of pulverizing it before he says, "The De Rozier alpha and his sister are already on their way here and you didn't think I might want to know?"

Carly adds in her alpha voice, "Donna. We'll discuss this in depth later."

Donna nods and offers a smile that reminds me of a child that has no remorse for eating all the ice cream. I hold back a giggle as she says, "Yes, of course, dear."

Annie glares at her. "Mother, come help me with the babies before you get yourself into more trouble."

When Donna stands to leave, she gives me a wink, and I can't help but grin at her. She had to give up her prima status to Carly and is now watching the control she has over this family slip from her fingers. But Donna has no intention of being silenced. And she shouldn't be. Her wisdom is a guiding force in this family, and while her approach tests Brady's patience, this clan would be lost without her.

I get up from the table to help with the babies, too. I plan to use Donna's rebellious streak to my benefit, because I'm dying to know more about Kimi and what hope lies ahead for keeping my children safe from Victor Veilleux.

CHAPTER 13

Lily

I DROP MY hand from my mouth yet again. When I was a kid, I used to bite my nails, and it's been years since I quit that nasty habit. But right now, tearing things with my teeth is keeping me from shifting and losing control as I wait to hear if Sierra's children are Victor's. I plop down on the overstuffed couch of the room that is now mine. The pink shades the decorator chose are lovely, and even though Victor suggested I redo this room to my taste, I didn't.

I glance over at my desk at the stack of book selections I'm reviewing for the summer reading program. The library and I have teamed up to encourage clan children to love books. But even my latest passion can't keep my mind off the impending news that weighs heavy on my mind, and any idea of working on the project while I wait disappears.

What was I thinking? I don't want to raise that woman's babies. I picture my husband holding an infant, and my heart warms as I imagine him as a father. Yes I do want to be a mother to his children. Because one of those triplets is the next Veilleux heir, and they're the bloodline of Victor. Besides, I'll make sure they grow up knowing right from wrong.

The town car engine hums in the distance, and I put down the pillow I was clutching to stand. I would send a telepathic message asking Victor what he found out, but he'll want to tell me in person. My Renaissance man doesn't even like to text. My hand flies to my mouth before I can stop myself, and I force it back down by my side. *Stop it, Lily.* No matter what he says, I'm going to make the best of the situation. That's what I do.

I take a deep breath and tug my shirt down. I walk to the door to greet my husband with a kiss. Victor walks in and locks his gaze on mine. He hands his briefcase without acknowledgement to the waiting butler as he moves quickly toward me. "Lily."

Worry fills me as he takes my face in his hands. I nod to indicate I know from his actions he is the father of Sierra's children. "It's okay, darling. We will handle this challenge with the dignity it deserves," I say.

My husband's shoulders relax, and he leans down to kiss me. "*You continue to amaze me. I swear you were born to make me a better person.*"

It would be so easy to lose myself in the sensations of my mate's mouth, but he needs reassurance from me. "*And you were born to complete me. I look forward to starting our family as soon as we can.*"

Victor pulls away, and his face becomes serious again.

"About that. We need to talk."

The familiar warmth of his hand envelops mine when I twine my fingers with his. "Come, you probably need a drink." Our feet thud with purpose as we make our way to his study, where I move to the wet bar. "Sit. I'll get you a whiskey."

My husband stands by the floor-to-ceiling window and gazes out at the expanse of snow-covered lawn. I sense there's more he's about to tell me, and I'm grateful my hands are busy pouring deep-amber liquid into our glasses, because I want to bite my nails again.

Ice cubes clink together as I walk over to him and hand him the drink. He takes it without turning to look at me. "When I was a little boy, I remember a time when my father had a difficult decision to make. He stood by the window of his study much like this one." Victor slips his arm around my waist as he takes a sip of his whiskey. "He told me that one day, I might have the weight of the clan on my shoulders and to never forget where we come from."

My stomach clenches in fear of what he's about to say to me. Is he about to shatter my world?

My mate kisses the top of my head, and I breathe a sigh of relief as he steps away from me to continue. "As werebear, we have duality to our lives. On the one hand, we are nurturing and value our humanity above everything else. But on the other, we are bear—fierce warriors that fight to protect what is ours."

"I want my children under this roof, and every ounce

of my being needs it to happen. But I made a grave mistake by biting Sierra first and creating this situation. If any member of the Veilleux clan was in my shoes, I would have to rule that the mother gets the children."

"What are you saying?"

"I've spoken with the Robichaux. In difficult situations between clans, we often bring in the leadership of a neutral clan to help mediate. Richard and Marion are suggesting joint custody."

The heat of anger rises in me. "No! One of those babies is the heir to this clan. Surely that matters? That child belongs with us, and since we can't know which one it is before puberty, we should get all three."

Victor has set down his glass, and he takes mine to do the same. It thumps lightly on the table, and I wonder how my husband can be so calm. "It most certainly does matter." His hands grip my arms, and I'm struck by the intensity of the heat radiating from his body when he says, "I'm not satisfied with the suggestion. I plan to inform the Le Roux they have a week to get those children to us."

"I don't understand. They aren't going to hand over the babies just because you said they must."

My mate releases me and steps back. "They won't. But if Sierra is gone, the children become mine."

"Gone?" *Oh my God.* The memory of Marion telling me Victor had kidnapped Sierra replays in my mind. Horror hits me, and I step back further as I shake my head. Ice runs through my veins. "No." I gaze over at my husband, and words come out of my mouth in a hoarse whisper, "You're going to take her?"

Victor's face softens as if I'm a scared child. His brow knits, and he says, "I'm going to eliminate her." My eyes must widen at the shock of what he means, because he steps close to me and grips my arms as if I might run. "Lily, don't you see? It must be done for the clan."

Tears prick my eyes at the idea my husband is planning murder. I can't condone that even if it means the Le Roux have a hand in the upbringing of my clan's next leader. I gaze up at Victor and watch the flicker of something silver in his eyes as his alpha voice says, "As prima, you'll stand by me in this decision. The heir to this clan is ours."

I nod slowly, because his power as prime over me is absolute. But I can't stop the tear that escapes from rolling down my face. If my husband is capable of murder, then maybe he did kidnap Carly and Sierra like I was told.

I remember how kind Carly was to me when I first saw her at our prima luncheon. I almost believed she meant it when she said all she ever wanted was for me to be happy. And Annie—*Oh God.*

Victor's voice breaks through my thoughts. "My darling, say something."

I realize he asked me a question, but I don't know what it was. "I'm sorry. What did you say?"

He cups my face in his hands and brushes the tear away with the pad of his thumb before he speaks softly. "I

CALLED BY THE BEAR - BOOK 3

asked if you would prefer I keep you out of matters such as these."

"Oh." I know what my husband wants to hear, and the same sense of self-preservation I called upon throughout my childhood rises to the occasion. I paste on a smile like so many times before as I find composure. "No. I just need to adjust to another new piece of my life. It's important for me to be informed if I'm to be by your side as a leader." I take a deep breath and stand taller, forcing him to drop his hands. "I told Patricia I would do what's necessary to be a good prima, and I meant it."

Victor lets out a large breath of air and reaches for our drinks. I force back the fear that threatens to give me away as he hands me my whiskey. He raises his glass to me. "To the strength to continue to make difficult decisions for the good of the Veilleux Clan."

Our crystal clinks with the toast, and the vision of glass shattering flashes through my mind. I swallow a large mouthful of whiskey but barely feel the sting. My fairy-tale life has just become a nightmare.

CHAPTER 14

Carly

T HE DOOR OF Ink It opens, and I glance up from my computer to see Lucy walking in. "Hey Lucy, how are you today?"

"Is Taylor here?"

I close my laptop with a click. "Yes. She's feeling better and came in to train you."

"Good." My sister walks over and seats herself on the couch. Her feet thud as she puts them on the coffee table. She picks up the same green binder of designs she looked at last week, the images she knows are mine. It makes me remember the conversation I had with Sierra. She said that Lucy draws well and that she seems to be interested in what it is we do here. I ask, "Do you have any tattoos?"

Lucy turns her attention to me. "No. I never really wanted one. They aren't my thing."

"I know what you mean. I only have the one that called me here."

Her eyes widen. "Don't people wonder why you don't have ink everywhere?"

"They do." I grin as I think about Sierra's two full sleeves of tattoos that spread over her shoulders, back, and chest. "Most assume Sierra is the artist and I'm the assistant."

"Why don't you have more than just your paw print?"

"I never wanted to have a tattoo I would regret. I needed it to mean something special." The skin on my wrist is smooth under my finger as I trace my tribal design.

"Is the call really that strong?"

I nod as I recall the dreams I used to have about Brady before I met him. I thought I was moving to Maine to meet a hot guy. And the bear in those visions? It wasn't something to be afraid of after all. It was my destiny. "Hey, after your workout today, I have a client scheduled. Would you like to come watch?"

"Maybe." Lucy bites her lip. "I mean, I guess so." Her hesitation makes me want to convince her.

"Sierra told me she saw your portfolio, and you're really good."

She picks an invisible piece of lint from her yoga pants. "I'm not so sure about that. I really just dabble in it."

"I'd love to see them. Would you let me look at your drawings, too?"

She stands up and tugs her T-shirt down. "Um, yeah. I've got to go work out."

I call out to her as she walks away. "My client will be

here at two o'clock."

Lucy's sneakers tap lightly across the concrete as she walks over toward Kick It. She turns back to look at me, and I smile. She gives me an awkward wave. I think I'm getting somewhere with her. While I don't expect us to be the best of friends, it would be nice to have a cordial relationship with my sister.

With time to kill before my next client, I decide to peek in on Lucy's training. Taylor has her practicing kicks. Her foot slaps repeatedly against the leather punching bag, impressing me with her flexibility, as Taylor instructs her to hit higher. After a few minutes, they move to the mats to spar. Lucy gains more of my respect with her speed and agility as she fights.

Movement behind me makes me think Ian has come over to join me, but I'm surprised to find Luke when I turn around. He cocks his eyebrows at me. "Spying?"

"Nope. Watching with admiration. Your trainers must be pretty decent if Lucy's skills are any indication."

My brother scowls for a moment but quickly smiles. "We managed just fine before you came along."

I hold up my hands. "Hey, this was your mother's idea. I'm not forcing anything on you."

Luke hits my arm lightly. "I'm joking. It's all good." He glances at Taylor and waggles his eyebrows. "There's something sexy about a woman that can fight. I don't mind one bit."

"Why do I get the feeling you have a line for every-thing?"

He winks at me as he walks backward toward the women. "Whatever gives you that idea?"

I chuckle and shake my head as he turns with a grin. I'm about to return to Ink It to prepare for my client when I notice Ian. His shoulders are slumped, and his head is in his hands as he leans over his desk. I make my way toward him.

"Ian. What's wrong?"

He looks up at me with sad eyes that make me want to pull him into my arms and offer comfort. "Annie and I are done."

I sink into the chair across from him and reach out to take his hand. "I'm so sorry. Why?"

"She can't live with the threat of my true mate coming along to break her heart, so she's breaking mine instead." He gets up and punches his palm with a growl. "This makes no sense!"

"Oh, Ian." I'm sure no words I have will help, so I don't bother with more.

Muscles along his arms ripple beneath his skin as he controls a shift. "I need to run."

I nod at him as he claws at his shirt to take it off. In his head I say, "*Go. I'll tell Taylor where you are.*"

He's barely out the back door before I hear his pained roar as he crashes into the woods. My thoughts turn to Annie, and I imagine she's suffering, too. I speak to her in my mind. "*Annie, I just saw Ian. Do you need some company?*"

"*How is he?*"

It's so typical of my sister-in-law to be worried about him instead of taking comfort when she needs it, too. *"Hurt and probably needs a good chick flick, ice cream, and wine. Like you. Plan to spend your evening on the couch with Sierra and me if she can get away. Okay?"*

"I'm—"

"You're not fine. Don't make me go alpha on you."

I picture Annie smiling when she telepathically messages me. *"Okay, see you later. Thanks, Carly."*

"You're welcome. I love you, Annie."

"I love you, too."

With that settled, I arrange my schedule so that Brady is taking the babies to Donna's. Sierra says she can get away, too. I was tempted to ask Taylor to join us because I really need to make an effort to include her in things, but knowing how close she is to Ian, I don't think it's appropriate.

I finish the plans just in time for my client. I welcome the distraction from the recent drama in my life, and when Lucy comes to watch, I'm so engrossed in my work that I almost don't notice. I stop my machine for a moment to introduce her and explain what I'm doing. The rhythmic process is mesmerizing, and my sister watches with an interest that seems to grow. By the end of the session, she's even asking questions.

The bell above the door jingles as my customer leaves. I turn to Lucy and guess from the smile on her face that she's hooked. "So what did you think?" I ask.

"That was awesome. You said your dad trained you,

right?"

"He did. And I taught Sierra." I'm afraid she's about to retreat, so I push forward. "If you think this is something you'd like to try, I can get you started."

My sister's face clouds over as if inner voices have started negative talk. "I don't know."

"Look. It's a huge thing. I get it. So why don't we start with you bringing me your portfolio, and I can give you direction with your sketches. Sound like a plan?"

Lucy has walked over to her gym bag and concentrates on the zipper as if it needs checking. "Sure. I'll bring it by."

I walk back toward my tattoo room to give her space. "Great. See you soon."

I leave her in the lobby without a need to say more. I watch as she continues to play it cool, but her body language gives her thoughts away when she swings her bag over her shoulder and almost skips out of Ink It. A grin covers my face as the odor of antiseptic floats in the air when I begin to clean my equipment. I think I just found a way to connect with my sister.

CHAPTER 15

Lily

M Y NAIL-BITING HABIT is back in full force, but that's the least of my worries. I'm married to a cold-blooded killer, and that trumps a manicure. Last night I sat through dinner with my husband pretending all was well. I kept trying to see the monster beneath his polished exterior, and little things gave him away. The way he cut his steak used to make me think of his strength, but last night I saw the anger. Even his voice, when he addressed Carol, struck a warning bell now that I know what he really is. *How could I have been so blind?*

I finally retreated to my drawing room with the excuse that I needed to finish up my plan for my library meeting today. What I really need to plan is how to keep Sierra alive. I may not love the girl, but she doesn't deserve to die so my husband can have his children. No matter how much I love Victor and no matter how important it is to gain custody of the babies, I cannot sit back and let him commit murder.

In addition to keeping an assassination from happening, I also need to learn the truth about my husband's relationship with Sierra. My gut is telling me that I may have been wrong about the Le Rouxs' intent and that it may not have been as evil as I have been led to believe. If only I knew who to trust.

"Ms. Lily, I've brought you some tea." I turn to Carol standing in the doorway with a tray. Her presence makes me aware of the fact I'm still in my pajamas and it's early afternoon.

"Oh. Did I ask for some? I'm sorry, I'm quite distracted today."

"You didn't, but I thought you might need it." Her gaze is kind as she leans over to set the tea down on my table, and I notice she included a couple of her macaroons. "Is there anything I can do for you?" she asks.

My throat thickens at her words, and I long to throw myself into her arms for a good cry. If only she were a loving version of my mother instead of one of the trusted Veilleux employees. I shake my head and wave her away, because I'm afraid words won't come out.

The faint scent of lemon rises from the hot liquid I pour into my cup. I wander to the window and glance out at the winter wonderland. Wind swirls snow from drifts into the air. Just yesterday I was daydreaming about Christmas in this beautiful mansion and planning how I would decorate for the holiday.

An icy tendril of fear slices through me when I remember how Victor wouldn't give me the key to the basement. He insisted it was filthy down there and he'd get Thomas to drag up the boxes of Christmas things. What would I find down there? Blood-red ribbons laced with a slice of steely silver? A more evil thought comes to me, and I wonder if there are secret dungeons or a torture chamber.

The tea is hot on my tongue when I take a sip, and I shake my horrible thoughts. I have a meeting with the librarian at four, and it won't bode well for the Veilleux if I don't make a good presentation. I sit and review my papers as I try to soothe my nerves with the sweet coconut flavor of Carol's cookies.

I WELCOME THE cold slap of wind on my face as I walk from the town car to the library entrance. It clears my head and lets me focus on the task at hand, which is more pleasant than where my mind has been most of today. The wooden floor beneath my feet creaks as I move across the expansive lobby area of the old building toward the front desk. My steps echo softly until I reach the area rug that muffles the noise.

A voice that is barely above a whisper says, "Mrs. Veilleux, I'm delighted to meet you."

I put out my hand to an older woman who has the perfect librarian bun complete, with gray streaked though brown color. Her eyes are rimmed in red, and I wonder if she might have been crying. "Please, call me Lily. It's a pleasure to meet you too, Mrs. Thompson."

"If I'm to call you Lily, I insist you call me Martha."

She turns on her flat shoes and leads me behind the counter. "Right this way. We can discuss things in my office."

A tissue swishes out of a decorative box, and she wipes her nose as I unbutton my tailored wool coat. She says, "Pardon me. I just received a bit of bad news, and I'm sure I look a mess."

I reach out to touch her arm. "Goodness, if this is a bad time, we can reschedule."

Martha holds out her hand to take my jacket. "Oh no. It's not every day I get to spend time with our prima. Please, sit."

I lower myself to a comfortable-looking chair across the desk from where she sits and recall Carol's kindness earlier today. "Martha, is there anything I can do?"

The woman sinks into her chair with a sigh. "Unfortunately, the damage is already done. I just learned that my niece's husband killed himself yesterday, and—" She stops and swallows as she blinks back fresh tears. "And it breaks my heart that my beautiful Amy had to go with him. She had such a bright future ahead of her." Martha's lips turn up a little when she confesses. "Amy planned to be a librarian like me."

"Oh, how tragic. She—?" I stop because I'm not sure whether Amy couldn't bear the loss and took her own life or her husband killed her too. Either way, I don't want to intrude.

Martha nods as if she knows what I was going to ask. "True mates. It's so senseless that when one partner dies, the other has to as well."

Wait, what? When a true mate dies, the other goes with them? Why didn't I know this? That doesn't sound right to me, and I make a mental note to find out more. "Oh, Martha. I'm so sorry for your loss."

She smiles at me through watery eyes as she dabs with a tissue. "Enough of this. Distract me with wonderful plans for clan children. I need a little happiness today."

I reach into my bag for my folder. "All right, but if you need me to stop at any time, just say the word."

It turns out planning the program was just what Martha needed, and she's even laughing a little at the stories she shares with me by the end of our meeting. I let our hug linger when I say goodbye, and we make plans to get together again next week.

When I leave the library, it's dark outside as the shortest day of the year in Maine approaches. I approach the silhouette of Thomas leaning against the town car, waiting. The temperature has dropped, and I welcome the warmth when I get in. My thoughts return to Martha's niece. "Thomas, can I ask you a question about true mates?"

"Yes, of course, Ms. Lily."

"I heard that when one true mate dies, the other does, too, but I find it hard to believe."

The blinker ticks softly as I wait for his reply. "That's not quite correct. It only happens when it's suicide."

"Oh, that's awful." I imagine the librarian's grief and guess it must be tainted with anger at the man who essentially killed her niece.

"Yes, it is."

I stare out the window at the faint outline of the forest illuminated by the headlights of passing cars. I trace a line in the fog on the window, revealing a sliver of black in the gray, and imagine being in a dark enough place that one would want to die knowing they'll kill their mate too. It hits me that I've just been given an option to save Sierra's life. While I would never take my own life, it's leverage I might be able to use.

My stomach clenches as I think about how I'm entertaining taking on Victor. But if I don't, he'll surely start a war that will kill innocent people and could very well wipe out a clan's alpha bloodline. The words of an old Native American woman I knew in Colorado echo in my mind. *"You are destined to save a clan."* Is this what she meant? That I was sent here to stop Victor? What if I'm supposed to save my husband instead? Heat rises to my face, and the car is suddenly stifling.

Thomas asks, "Ms. Lily, is everything okay?"

I glance in the rearview mirror at his reflection dimly lit by the dashboard and force myself to breathe deeply. I offer a forced smile. "Everything's fine."

The driver chuckles softly before he says, "Good. Because your husband loves life more than anyone I know. He won't be killing himself soon."

I grin back at him. Little does he know I'm not worried about my life, because I'm plotting how to stop his alpha. "Glad to hear it, because I've got big plans."

Thomas's tone becomes somber when he says, "I'm sure you do, Mrs. Veilleux. I'm sure you do."

CHAPTER 16

Carly

I WALK INTO my home and the aroma of baked goods. I head straight to the kitchen to find a small feast's worth of goodies on the table. The plastic of my shopping bags filled with chips, dip, and wine rustles when I set them down next to the peanut butter cookies, German chocolate cake, and pecan pie. "Wow. Sierra's going to be in sugar heaven."

Annie turns to me, and I notice flour on her cheek. "Yeah. I bake when I'm upset." She's holding a spatula with a chocolate chip cookie on it and extends her hand toward me. "Want one?"

I take the warm offering and bite into oozing heaven. A shameless moan escapes my lips before I swallow the mouthful down. "I'm not going to stay at pre-baby weight, am I?"

"Nope, not until I get over my heartache."

I walk over and hug her. "I wish alpha powers let me wave a magic wand to make your Prince Charming materialize."

"That would be a neat trick." Annie steps away from me, and her eyes fill with moisture. "Can you conjure up a princess for Ian, too?"

"Oh, honey." I pull her back to me. "Let it out. A little snot on my shoulder is nothing compared to what the babies do every day."

Annie chuckles before the laughter turns to sobs. I imagine she's crying about more than her love life, though. As strong as she is everyday, she'll never get the one thing she wants: children of her own. No matter how close she is to my children, it has to be painful to know she'll never be a mother.

If only I could fix part of this. I want to tell her another true mate will come along and she just needs to be patient. But I can't promise something like that when we don't even know if it can happen. Instead, I hold my dear sister-in-law and offer what small comfort I can. Her hair is silky under my fingers as I stroke it, and she tries to let the pain of heartbreak bleed away.

When she's done, she pulls away. "I should make ice cream."

I smile in response, because while I'm sure Sierra will arrive with enough supplies to make hot fudge sundaes for an army, Annie can't help herself. "I'll go cue up the cry movies. Any preferences?"

"Nope. Just make sure there's plenty of tissues handy."

I'm clicking through movies available with our online subscription when Sierra arrives. She stops to read through the list. "God, those are all so depressing." She moves toward the kitchen as she calls out, "Put some comedy in there, too. We're going to need it."

I laugh when I hear her squeal over the whine of the ice cream maker. "I've died and gone to bakery heaven! Forget men, Annie. Marry me."

I reach for the bowl of chips when the noise of the machine stops, and I say, "I'll marry the first person to bring me wine."

Annie leans over me from behind the couch and hands me a goblet full of pale-yellow liquid. "Already on it." She comes around to sit next to me and places a tray full of sweets on the table with a clatter.

She looks at my list on the TV screen. "Let's start with *Steel Magnolias*. It's Donna's favorite, and I remember watching it with her when I was a kid."

"What a coincidence. My dad brought home the DVD to watch when my first boyfriend broke up with me." I wonder if it was one of Marion's favorite movies.

"What a sweet man. Did he cry along with you?"

I nod and tear up a little at the memory of my father trying to be the mother I didn't have. "He did. People thought of him as a tough guy, but he knew how to be a softie when it came to me."

Sierra makes the couch bounce when she lands on Annie's other side. "Al was the best. Remember when he was sick and we painted his toenails so the surgeon would wonder about him? I thought he was going to get thrown out of the hospital for laughing so loudly."

I don't want to think about how I lost my father to lung cancer, so I lean into Annie and change the subject. "I bet your dad was pretty special, too."

"He was. But I don't want to cry again just yet. Let's watch the movie."

By the time Brady arrives home, we've gorged ourselves on sugar, salt, and alcohol. I stop the movie we aren't watching so we can turn our attention to my husband when he sits on the coffee table to talk to us. "Donna will be by in the morning with the triplets, and we'll discuss this at our meeting, but I want to share her news with you now."

Sierra perks up, and I ask, "What's going on?"

"She spoke to Kimi, and we may get a compromise I think everyone can live with." He glances at Sierra. "As much as I wish we could keep Victor from seeing your children, we can't, because one will be the next Veilleux alpha. But we can keep them safe."

My best friend crosses her arms and tilts her head at Brady as if she's skeptical. He continues. "Kimi plans to meet with their medicine man, and they'll spell the children so that if any harm comes to them or their parents, the consequences will be grave enough to keep everyone in check."

Annie asks, "What exactly are the consequences?"

"It hasn't been decided yet, but I have no doubt they'll be severe."

Sierra scoots forward on the couch. "So Ashton and I will be safe, and so will Lily and Victor?"

"That's my understanding. I'm sure we'll get more information after Kimi and Tokala meet."

I don't want to say it out loud, so I speak to my mate privately. *"There are a hundred ways this could go wrong, aren't there?"*

"I'm afraid so."

"This is good news. I'm sure we'll figure out an acceptable compromise," I say.

Sierra gets up. "I'm not going to like anything other than Victor never laying a finger on my babies. I think I need more wine." She asks Brady, "Want a glass?"

He sighs. "Yes. I don't like this any more than you do." He takes Sierra's place on the couch and wraps an arm around Annie's shoulders. "How's my sister?"

She leans against him. "I've had better days. But I'll manage."

"Maybe you should try a human man."

Annie hits his arm, and Sierra hands him his drink as she says, "No way, they can't compare. I'd rather be alone."

Brady raises his eyebrows at me. "Is that true?"

Annie's eyes light up. "Is this about dicks again? Because Donna will be sorry she's not here."

"It's so much more than the unusually large size of the werebear love stick. It's what they do with it." Sierra places herself on the coffee table to face us.

Brady snorts out wine. "Love stick?"

Sierra leans forward and speaks in a suggestive tone as her hands add a visual to the words, "Silken rod, steely memb—"

My husband holds out his hand. "Stop! What ever happened to using the word 'cock'?"

"Or 'penis.'" Annie giggles uncontrollably.

Brady's eyes crinkle at the corners as he tries to be stern. "I think you ladies have had a little too much to drink."

"Or not enough. Maybe it's time for shots," Sierra adds. "And then I'll tell you more about the difference between human and werebear men."

I jump in before Sierra takes us to a scary place. "Oh no. Some things are better left unsaid."

Sierra pretends annoyance. "Fine." She leans in to Annie and whispers loudly. "I'll tell you later."

Annie pats her knee as she yawns. "I have no doubt."

Brady asks Sierra, "Are you staying here tonight?"

"Nope, Ash is already on his way to get me."

He teases her. "Tell me the fun isn't over already?"

"Sorry, big guy, I've got another man to torture." She winks at my husband. "But I bet your wife can find a way to keep you busy."

Annie gets up and stretches before reaching for dishes. I say, "Don't. I'll take care of everything."

Sierra stands and hugs her. "You're one of the bravest and kindest souls I know. You deserve happiness, and I'm sure it will come for you."

"Thanks." My sister-in-law kisses her on the cheek. "Now if you don't mind, I'm going to go to bed. I'm exhausted and ready to end this day."

As Annie climbs the stairs, I get up to gather our snacks to bring to the kitchen. Brady joins me in the task. I recall the dream I had last night about Annie and a man with hair so blond it was almost white. Hoping my vision was a premonition, I smile.

Maybe love is in Annie's future after all.

CHAPTER 17

Sierra

THE SUV IS toasty warm, and the faint odor of Ashton's musk is present, tantalizing my werebear senses. "How's Ian?" While girls' night was happening at the Le Roux house, Ashton was hosting a male version for his brother.

"He's handling the breakup rather well. We shot some pool with Taylor, and he only had one beer. I think he's seen this coming for a while now."

"Yeah, we all have." Soft country music is playing on the radio, and I imagine it's a song that could fit the situation. "When I first learned about mates and how werebear rarely worry about each other's feelings, I thought you were lucky. But the whole true mate thing can really suck."

Ashton reaches over and takes my hand. His calloused fingers rub against my skin. "But when we find each other, it's perfect."

It is. My love for Ashton is absolute, and I know his for me is the same. I lift his hand and kiss the palm.

"Have I told you lately how amazing you are?"

"You don't have to. That's the beauty of us."

"True, but don't you like to hear it?" I suck the tip of his finger and slide it out of my mouth slowly. "Don't you like to know that you're the star of my sexual dreams?"

My husband moans as my lips flutter down the underside of his forearm. "I do."

I twist in my seat to reach over and kiss his neck. I speak so my breath is on his skin. Because Ian is the babysitter and is staying over, I decide I'll please my husband somewhere I don't have to worry about us being overheard. "Can I live out one of my fantasies before we get home?"

Ash shifts in his seat, and I place my hand on his crotch to press against his growing erection. "I think that can be arranged."

His skin is salty under my tongue when I drag it down to the coarse hair on his chest. It's been a month since I had the babies, and I shouldn't have penetrative sex, but that doesn't mean I can't make my husband scream. "You should probably pull over for what I have in mind." The metal button on his jeans pops open, and the grind of his zipper roars quietly as I pull it down slowly.

"Right. We'll be on our road in a minute."

I grip the silky-smooth skin of his hard cock and guide it out of his pants. Moisture beads up on the tip, and I rub my thumb over it as I undo my seat belt with a click. "I'm not sure I can wait."

I scramble up to my knees on my seat and lower my head to his lap. I lick a circle around the head of his dick. "I must taste you."

"Sweet Jesus, Sierra." Ashton's hips buck up to thrust himself deeper into my mouth. "I'm still driving."

"Um hmm." The vibration of my humming must feel good, because my husband is trembling beneath me when he finally slows down and pulls into the turnaround at the end of our driveway. He manages to shift the car into park. I suck hard and remove my mouth with a slurp. "Finally." I reach over and remove his seat belt, too. "Now where was I?"

Ashton fists my hair and pulls me up to his mouth. "You were blowing my mind." He kisses me hungrily, and I have to use force to pull away to get back to my plan.

"And you. I thought this was my fantasy." With my mate's hands still gripping my hair, I return to my oral ministration. He pulls my head gently to delve into my mouth deeper. The low rumble of his bear sounds in my ears, and I work at bringing him to the brink of a climax. Sweet release fills my senses as his growl becomes a roar, and then he slumps in his seat.

"Got any more ideas we need to fulfill?"

I wipe my mouth on my sleeve as I sit up. "I've got plenty, but I'm going to let you savor that one for a while."

A content sigh whooshes out of Ash. "I will." He lifts his hips to refasten his jeans. "Maybe you should drive."

I snicker. "Again. I think I just did."

My mate reaches over and pulls me to his chest to nuzzle my neck. "You know, this could become our make-out spot. You can scream as loud as you want and not wake up the kids."

"You might be onto something. I have a lot of car fantasies left."

My nipples harden as my husband moves lower, fluttering kisses on my sensitive breasts. The vibration of his voice tickles when he mumbles, "Me too."

Rustling in the woods captures my attention, and I open my eyes to see two glowing ones return my stare. Is that another werebear? "Shit!"

Ash turns to look out the window where I'm pointing, but whatever it was is gone. "What?"

I shake my head. "I thought I saw someone"—the image I recall wasn't what I imagine bear or human eyes would look like—"or something watching us."

Before I finish speaking, my husband has already opened the door of the SUV. He gets out to listen and sniff for a scent. Panic sets in, and my skin pricks with the beginnings of my shift. "The babies!"

I bolt out of the car as fabric tears along my chest. I don't stop to deal with it as I race up toward the house in bear form. *Shit!* I can't open the door with my paws, and it's reinforced with steel, making it impossible to break down.

Ashton is right next to me and shifting back to human form, so I let him turn the handle, and I push through to the nursery. A quick glance at Ian standing by the couch with a confused look should lessen my fear, but it isn't until I see three sleeping infants in their cribs that I begin to calm down. Within a minute, I've returned to my usual self, and I pad over to kiss each baby.

My mate joins me and whispers, "They're fine."

I lift my shaking hand to his cheek and speak in his mind. *"This time. But something evil was in the woods. I can feel it."*

"I'll take care of it." Ashton includes me in his telepathic message. *"Send a team. Someone was on my land tonight, and Sierra won't sleep until we find out who it is and deal with them accordingly."*

A sad realization hits me. My children are no longer safe in our home, and I can't avoid the need for bodyguards any longer. I turn to Ian standing in the hallway and approach him as I whisper, "Downstairs." I continue to my room to grab robes for Ash and me.

I make my way down to the living room and to my husband and his twin. "Ian, I saw something in the woods at the bottom of our driveway." I glance quickly at Ash before I continue. "It was probably a bear, but there was something strange about the eyes. They were sort of glowing like—I don't know." I shake my head. "Anyway, as much as I hate this, I think it's time for stricter security."

My husband wraps his arms around my shoulders and pulls me close. "Good. I'll feel so much better knowing you and the babies are protected when I'm not around."

I inhale the scent of the man I couldn't live without. "It wouldn't be a bad idea if you have protection, too."

Ashton gazes down at me. His brows knit as he studies my face. "If it would make you feel safer, I'll do it."

My arms wrap around his waist, and I hug him tight. "Thank you. Until this is over, I don't think we can be too careful."

Even though we heard them coming, Ashton's coworkers knock at the door. I give my husband a quick kiss while Ian lets the men in, and I return upstairs to let them do their thing. Before retreating to my bedroom, I walk over and touch each of my children as if I need to know they're really there. Tears prick my eyes as I imagine the horrors that could have occurred had we not scared off the evil. I pray the medicine woman Kimi knows what she's doing, because I need an end to this nightmare.

CHAPTER 18

Lily

YOU CAN CERTAINLY dress up the girl from across the tracks, but you can't take away the urge to hit the mall. Especially when it comes to jeans. Finding ones that fit my curvy body is tough, and I'm faithful to the brand that works.

As the town car leaves Veilleux land, I breathe a sigh of relief. I could use a dose of the human world that used to be my normal and forget my drama for a little while. A horn sounds when we enter the mall road, and I watch an angry driver flip off the guy who didn't wait his turn at the stop sign. Frazzled holiday shoppers make me grateful Thomas can drop me at the entrance.

"There's no need for you to try to follow me around the mall, Thomas. I can fend for myself quite well in the human world."

The car pulls up along the sidewalk, and the engine clunks into park. The driver's gray eyes twinkle as he turns to look at me. "I have no doubt. You can call my cell when you're ready to be picked up."

Thomas gets out and opens my door. I take his hand and ask, "Can I get you anything? There's a lovely chocolatier, and I'm happy to grab some for your wife."

"You read my mind, Ms. Lily. Don't you worry about it, though. I was planning on getting some while you shop."

"Well, all right, then." I pull my coat tighter around myself for the quick walk to warmth. "Thank you."

"My pleasure, Ms. Lily."

Heat blasts at me loudly when I enter the first door, and I escape to the more subdued noise of the mall through the second. Of course, I forgot about the volume humans need music to be, and a Christmas song about chestnuts on an open fire blares in my ears. I stand for a minute to adjust and reacquaint myself with my old world.

I wander past children squealing in an automobile-themed play area and avoid the kiosk salesman who asks if I want a free sample of rejuvenating hand cream from the Dead Sea. I smile, wondering if he gets the irony.

Up ahead, I see the familiar turquoise sign of my favorite jean shop. The odor of perfume I assume is meant to make me want to purchase more accosts me when I enter. At least the lighting is good and the music isn't so loud I can't think. I'm glad I chose the middle of a workday to shop, because I seem to be the only customer in the store. A woman approaches me and recites her current sales speech. She tells me her name is Mallory and to ask her for help if I need it.

I smile and thank her for the information. Worn denim is soft under my fingers as I browse through the display of jeans looking for my size. When I find it, I grab one of every design to try on. I search for Mallory so she can let me into the dressing room.

She leads me to a section that is quiet compared to the rest of the store. When she clicks open a lock, I realize I'm no longer alone. My sensitive hearing picks up the soft sound of a woman crying. I slip off my shoes and wonder what might be wrong.

The slacks I remove swish softly to the floor. I begin the process of wiggling into a pair of pants. When I fasten the button, I can't ignore my worry any longer. I call out to the woman in the dressing room next to me, "Are you okay?"

She sniffs. "Yeah. It's silly, I'm not sure why I'm crying."

Is that Annie? Determined not to make the situation awkward, I joke. "Let me guess. You got a good look at your backside in these mirrors, because that always makes me cry."

She chuckles. "Lily? Is that you?"

"It is. Hi, Annie."

There's a period of silence as I recall the last thing I said to her was to never contact me again. "Hey, just so you know, I don't hate you."

The door to Annie's dressing room creaks open. "I've missed you."

I push my door open and step out to face her. "I've

really missed you too." My friend's cheeks are blotchy from crying, and I step forward to pull her into a hug. "I don't know what's wrong, but if I can do anything to help, I will."

Annie relaxes in my arms. "There isn't a thing you can do. I'm crying over a relationship I knew was doomed from the start." She steps back. "After you left, Ian and I got together. Only it was a mistake, because his true mate is out there somewhere, and it's only a matter of time before they find each other. I left him before he could break my heart." She takes a shaky breath. "Apparently I was too late."

"Oh, Annie. I'm so sorry." I know my friend has lost her true mate and that she'll never get that kind of love again.

She waves her hand. "So cheer me up. Tell me about your new life."

My face falls before I remember to hide my feelings. "I live in a huge mansion with servants that cater to my every need. I have an unlimited to budget to buy anything I want and a husband that is my true mate." I shrug. "It's glorious."

Annie squints at me. "So what's wrong?"

A sofa and chair are set out in the dressing room area, and I plop onto the plush couch. Annie and I hit it off the first day we met, and she's the closest girlfriend I've had in a long time. My instincts tell me I can trust her even if she belongs to our rival clan. "I have questions, and I don't know who to ask."

The cushion sinks as Annie sits next to me. "I've never lied to you, Lily, and I won't start now. Ask me anything."

"Can you tell me what you know about what happened between Victor and Sierra?" I close my eyes and shake my head a little because she's likely been fed a party line from the other side. "I mean, can you tell me anything you actually saw with your own eyes?"

"Sure. I didn't witness Victor bite Sierra at Carly and Brady's wedding, but Carly must have, because she screamed in our heads when it happened and then made Keith bite her, too. Within minutes, Sierra started to change."

I recall the agony of the process, and I grimace, thinking about how I didn't know what was happening. "Did she know she was changing?"

"Yes. She has seen it happen to Carly." Annie takes my hand. "After she became a werebear, Victor and Keith could both talk in her head. While I couldn't hear what Victor was saying, whatever it was it upset Sierra to the point she lost weight, had to quit her job, and eventually broke up with Keith over it."

I imagine what it would be like to have a voice in my head that I couldn't shut up. I shudder when I think of the things an alpha command could make me do. Annie's face is full of concern when she asks, "Do you want to hear about the kidnapping?"

My stomach rolls, and I ask the question even though I dread the answer. "Are you sure she was kidnapped?

Maybe she went willingly."

Annie shakes her head. "The day it happened, Sierra was in an unusually good mood, because she said Victor was leaving her alone. She and Carly shifted and ran through the woods to Fishing Gorge for a swim. A little while later, Carly messaged us that people were shooting at them and they needed help."

Oh, God. Did Victor order his men to kill them? Why?

Annie continues. "When help got there, the women were nowhere to be found. We were frantic for days trying to locate Carly and Sierra." My friend bites her lip, and I guess she's recalling the anguish of that time. "Eventually Carly managed to contact Brady, and she was found in the woods. She had no idea how she got there, but she remembered being in a cage and Sierra talking in her head. I don't know what was said, but the assumption was made that Victor was keeping Sierra prisoner."

"How did you know it was Victor and not someone else?"

Annie looks at me with resignation. "Our clans' history hasn't been very peaceful, and Victor bit Sierra for a reason. We assumed he wanted her."

Victor's teary eyes flash in my mind as I replay his confession of weakness around Sierra and her charms. I'm not willing to give anything away, so I ask, "But didn't she want to be with him because of the mate bond?"

"Yes. She probably did."

Hope finds its way into my heart. "So it's possible she

stayed willingly, right?"

"It is. But she said there were guards that prevented her from leaving."

I think about all the men who patrol my grounds to keep me safe. It wouldn't be hard for them to keep me from leaving, either.

Marion's words come back to me. "*You might also want to know that Sierra was rescued on the Fourth of July.*" I ask, "What day was Sierra found?"

"The Fourth of July. I'm sure of it because the mission was planned knowing Victor would be at the celebration."

Bile rises to my throat. Marion was right. The day after the Fourth was when my mate insisted on seeing me. We got engaged that night and married the next day. Was he covering his tracks? Replacing Sierra? Whatever it was, the man I love beyond measure lied to me then, and he still does.

Annie interrupts my thoughts. "One more thing. Sierra went willingly with her rescuers. If she was there voluntarily, that wouldn't have happened."

My head is swimming with what I've learned, and I need to get out of here. "I've got to go." I stand and yank the tag on my jeans with a snap. "Annie, it was good to see you." I snatch the hangers of pants from the dressing room with the intention of buying them all and slip on my shoes. When I bend down to retrieve the rest of my clothes, I say, "I'm not sure I can call you, because—"

Annie says, "I know." She grabs my arm as I move to

walk by. "If you need me for anything, I'll do whatever I can. Carly would, too. Understand?"

"Yeah." I pull away. "Thanks."

By the time I've paid and called Thomas, I'm pounding down the mall hallway in anger. Victor has a lot of explaining to do, and this time I won't be falling for what he thinks I want to hear.

CHAPTER 19

Carly

PLATES AND GLASSES rattle as Annie shuts the dishwasher, and she says, "It's not like Keith to be so late. What do you think is going on?"

Our weekly morning meeting has been delayed waiting for Taylor and Keith, so we focused on eating instead. "I don't know. He told me Taylor went for a run early this morning, and he thought maybe she lost track of time," I say.

"Taylor's too familiar with the forest to get lost," Ashton says. "Didn't their guard see which way she went? Maybe she got hurt."

Coffee splashes into a mug as Brady refills his cup. "Keith said she went her usual way, and he hasn't heard anything. She's not answering my communications, either."

My stomach sinks, because there's no good reason she wouldn't have heard them. I ask, "Should we send out a search team?"

Ashton has Jackson in his arm like a football and

rocks him as he replies. "Yes. Considering we think the Veilleux might have tried to sabotage Taylor in her own home, I'd rather not take any chances."

Brady nods, and I hear his alpha order to our warriors.

Donna says, "We might as well get started. They can get caught up later." She reaches for the teapot and takes her time preparing her drink as we all get settled for the meeting. "Shall we begin with the custody situation?"

Sierra's face gets solemn as she nods.

"My meeting with Kimi went well," Donna says. "She agreed that the babies will have to split time between both clans for their formative years but thinks she can cast a spell that will keep them safe."

"Did she say what that spell will involve?" Sierra shreds a napkin slowly.

"No. But none of this is a done deal until the prime and prima of each clan sign off on it."

I reach over and stop Sierra's hands. "I know this is hard, but Brady and I won't agree to anything that would endanger your children."

My friend nods, and her eyes glisten with unshed tears. My heart breaks a little as I imagine her anguish.

Annie speaks up. "Lily will make sure of it, too. I ran into her at the mall, and she had a lot of questions about you, Sierra. I think she may be doubting the intentions of her true mate."

While I knew about Annie talking to Lily, Sierra didn't, and she says, "But Victor is an alpha, and he can order her to go along with anything he says."

I wince at her words, because after being forced to stay with him in a mate bond, she knows better than anyone how that works.

Annie replies, "That's true. But she's not held against her will. She may be quiet, but I've seen her negotiate like a pro."

I add, "And according to Marion, Victor is changing for the better because of Lily. All of us have experience with how true mates work. He won't go completely against her wishes, because he can't."

Ashton grins. "Good point. Have you seen my throw pillows?"

Sierra's face loosens into a small smile at his teasing, and she turns to Annie. "Does she know everything?"

"She knows enough to doubt what Victor told her." Annie reaches over and swipes the torn bits of napkin across the table and into her palm. "Lily is a good person, so I think she'll fight for the right thing."

Donna squints at Annie as if she's not so sure. She says, "Moving on. The De Roziers, Tristan and Isabelle, are arriving in a few days. They'll be staying here thanks to Annie, Brady, and Carly's generosity."

Brady snorts. "And because you want them to be monitored at all times."

"Let's just say I want to know more about them and why they want our help." Donna sips her tea slowly.

"If they're going to bring us women to create more Le Roux, then I think we need to find a way to help them out." I wink at Sierra. "While I'm sure your current breeders will provide a few more children, we need as many as we can get."

Donna says, "Don't rule out others coming from the call. It hasn't gone away, and as fertile descendants in the human world become adults, they may be compelled to answer."

Lucy's friend Tori comes to mind, and I recall how she could see my paw print. "I think one might already be here. Lucy brought a friend into Ink It a while back, and she was interested in my tattoo."

Donna rubs her hands in glee. "I knew it. Come spring, she'll be unable to resist." She purses her lips in thought and then says, "I wonder who's dreaming about her."

Annie shakes her head as she chuckles. "Mother, you might consider opening up a dating service. You get way too excited about these things."

My mother-in-law grins. "You sure about that? Because I'd force you to be my first client."

Annie banters back. "You know, it might be time for you to start dating. How did you put it?" She taps her lip as we start to laugh. "Ah, yes. You need to get some good loving; it would make you less concerned about the rest of us."

Brady groans, but he's smiling. "Really? Now it's my turn to say 'moving on.' Let's get back to the De Roziers." Once everyone sobers, he says to Donna, "Give us some history."

"They're a clan from the Arctic. Over the years, they've lost a fair number of members to the human population, as most of the land was gambled away by the late De Rozier alpha. There's also the issue of global warming, and the polar werebear has had to adapt to warmer temperatures. Tristan just came into power, and I've heard he's no slouch."

Brady asks, "The original plan for getting their help was to merge our clans?"

"Correct, but Tristan's father wanted no part of it. Seems he was a bit closed minded over the idea of interracial relationships."

"Wait, would they have come here to live?" asks Sierra.

Donna answers, "That was an option we presented but not a requirement."

"That would make three alphas in the combined clan." Ashton's deep voice adds to the seriousness of the statement.

Brady's coffee mug thumps on the table with a little more force than necessary as he frowns. "Or they could remain a separate clan and we offer them land to relocate."

"So many options. I say we wait until we get to know Tristan and Isabelle before we form a plan," says Annie.

I stand to sway back and forth with a fidgety Elliot. "Agreed. I'm not comfortable making any decisions until we get a handle on just who the De Rozier twins really are."

Annie settles a sleeping Audrey in a bassinet while Sierra asks, "Hey, how old is this Tristan?"

Donna says, "Young. Early twenties, I think."

"Oh, Annie, what if he ends up being smokin' hot? Talk about the perfect distraction." Sierra winks at my sister-in-law.

Annie giggles and says, "I wonder if he has a nice love stick."

Donna's eyes widen at her daughter's words. "Are you talking about dicks?"

Sierra says, "Yup. We've totally corrupted her. Right, Carly?"

I hold up my hands. "I'm not taking credit for that. It's all on you."

Brady looks at Ashton. "Things are going downhill fast." He turns to the rest of us. "I assume we're done here?"

"Yes," replies Donna. "The only other topic to discuss was the possibility of Victor causing the accident at Taylor and Keith's. But that needs to wait until they're present."

I speak in Brady's head. *"Any word on Taylor?"*

"No. And I'm quite concerned." Brady nods toward Ashton. "We should go help with that."

He kisses me quickly. *"I'll keep you in the loop."*

My gut is telling me that something is very wrong, and I call out to Taylor. *"Hey, we're looking for you, and Brady, Keith, and I won't stop listening. Hang on."*

Once the men leave, Sierra asks, "What do you think

Victor wants with Taylor? She's fierce, and if any one of us could escape his clutches on their own, it would be her."

"I don't know, but Keith sure can't catch a break. He's got to be frantic over this," says Annie.

I reach my hand out to my sister-in-law, and she grips it tight enough to hurt. Talk about someone who can't catch a break. Annie wants babies more than anything but is barren due to an ancient curse. Her father and true mate were killed by the Veilleux, and she can't even find love that doesn't come with strings attached.

I reach my other hand out to Sierra, who is living her own nightmare having to share custody of her children with a monster. I glance at Donna when she grabs onto Sierra and Annie, too. She says, "We'll find Taylor and defeat Victor. I know it's hard to believe right now, but the prophecies are playing out the way they are supposed to." She gazes intently into my eyes. "You'll save this clan, Carly. It's your destiny."

CHAPTER 20

Taylor

M Y HEADLIGHTS BOUNCE from the bumps in the snow-covered dirt road leading away from Ashton and Sierra's house. Love sucks. And so does the true mate thing. The idea that you can be head over heels for someone only to have it disappear in an instant when you meet your true mate is a cruel joke. But I'm told werebears think the human world's cheating problem is pretty crappy, too.

After a few games of pool at Ashton's house, I'm on my way home to Keith. I'm confident Ian is okay with Annie dumping him. Even though it hurts, she let him know early on she couldn't commit with the threat of his true mate being out there to steal him away some day. I crank up the heat in my truck and hold my hand up to the vent to warm my fingers.

I'm barely past Ashton's driveway when a slicing pain in my head makes my vision blurry. It's so hard to see that I pull over. My flashers tick when I push the button, and I close my eyes.

The familiar woman with long dark hair is standing in a nursery. Three cribs surround her, and she beckons me closer. I move slowly so I don't wake the babies. Just as I'm about to be able to see their faces, she orders me to halt. She says, "You know what you must do." I try to remember, but I'm confused. The woman speaks again. "Bring them to me."

Suddenly I'm trudging in snow and parting branches to make my way through the woods. A large house is up ahead, and light glows from a window. I need to get inside. Noise startles me, and I crouch down low so I'm not discovered. I glance over to find a car and its passenger staring right at me. I turn and run.

A knock on my truck window wakes me. I blink a few times and realize my vision is back to normal. I must've fallen asleep. I hit the button to lower the window and speak to the man outside. He asks, "Need some help?"

"No. I'm fine. I just needed to rest my eyes a bit before continuing."

"Smart girl. Drive safe now."

My feet are cold, and after I turn up the heat, I notice the bottoms of my jeans are wet. How strange. I wonder how that happened. I shake my head and decide I must not have remembered walking through snow to get to my truck when I left Ashton's house. Since when did I get so spacy?

GETTING UP IN the middle of the night is becoming a

usual thing. Another dream woke me, and while I can't remember most of it, I recall the tall, thin woman who's haunting me. I'm trying to figure out how I know her, because I'm sure I do. I gaze out at the moonlight filtering through the fairyland forest Keith cultivated beyond the wall of glass in our living room. I wish I could remember her face more clearly.

My teakettle is hissing, and I hurry into the kitchen to take it off the stove before it whistles and wakes my husband. I need to drink my tea and can't risk him figuring out it's not chamomile like the label says.

After I make my hot beverage, I return to the living room. I take a mouthful, knowing that scalding my tongue is better than tasting the fertility blend once it cools down. The moon has sunk lower in the sky, and the hint of dawn paints the landscape into shades of gray. The rush of water in pipes from the toilet flushing tells me Keith is up. He'll hop in the shower next, and I'm about to go make him coffee when something catches my eye.

Movement in the trees quickens my pulse, and my intuition tells me it's the woman in my dreams. Even though I'm barefoot, I unlock the back door next to the glass wall and step outside to get a better look. Snow is cold under my feet with the first few steps, and it begins to get painful as I move farther into the forest. I just need to find her...

My human form is shivering, and I shift into a bear for warmth. As bones crack, Keith's voice calls me. I send him a message. "I'm off for a run, babe. I'll be back later." I begin to move before my transformation is complete, but I'm fast, and within a few steps I'm on all fours, with power exploding from my sinewy legs. As I turn the corner of my usual route, the flowing fabric of a long coat appears in the distance.

Her voice taunts me. "Come. I have something to show you." But no matter how desperate I am to catch the woman, she remains out of reach. It's as if she's flying along the ground. At the point I'm sure I'll collapse from exhaustion, we reach a gorge. The emerald-green fabric of her coat balloons up as the woman jumps off the cliff, and I don't hesitate to follow her.

I splash into water that the tender membranes in my nose detect as icy, but the cold doesn't penetrate my fur. I'm led deep into the river and through a faintly lit hole that reminds me of a portal in sci-fi movies. Swimming quickly under the water, I'm in desperate need of air, and my lungs burn. Before I can panic, we pop up into a dark area that might be a cave, because the splashing echoes around me.

The dank odor of dead leaves and mold fills my nostrils as I gasp for oxygen. Streaks of light slice through the dark, and my eyes adjust to reveal the woman on the edge of the pool of water. Her feet are dangling in it, and she pats the edge for me to join her. I swim over and climb out with great effort, because my body's energy is spent.

I would shift, but being naked in winter temperatures

isn't a good idea, so I lie down next to the person I've been following. The faint sound of Keith calling me echoes in the distance, but I block out the words as she strokes my head. "Rest. We have so much to talk about, and I'll need you alert for it."

I nod, because I'm too tired to even growl. My eyes shut, and I sink into a deep sleep.

I SNAP AWAKE as if I'm not supposed to be sleeping. *What the hell?* Why am I in bear form? I lift up and realize I'm on a hard rock floor, and I'm surrounded by the bitter cold of being deep in the frozen earth where sunlight never shines. I have a foggy memory of running through the forest, following the familiar woman.

As my eyes adapt to the near darkness, I notice a pile of clothing and move toward it to paw through the items. It's gear designed for winter outdoor activity. I guess I'm supposed to shift and put it on. I'd have been hesitant if this had happened months ago, but since I was called to Maine and met Keith, I have no doubt that this is what I'm supposed to do.

As soon as I'm human, my body hates me for it as the cold makes me shiver. I pull on the fleece long underwear quickly, and nylon swishes over my legs as I yank up snow pants. Once I'm dressed, I begin to search for a way out of the cave. As I navigate the perimeter, a draft signals an opening, and I find a narrow passageway that requires I turn sideways to fit through. Fortunately, it isn't long before my path widens, and I'm not forced to slide against God knows what that's stuck on the moist walls.

As I wind around corners, the light brightens until I spy an exit. The hole to climb out is small, and I have to squeeze through, catching my hair on twigs and brush that block the way. When I stand, I'm on the edge of a snow-covered field and discover a small cottage on the other side. Smoke is rising from the chimney, and my stomach growls when the scent of bacon travels toward me.

My clunky knee-high boots wouldn't keep me dry if I had to break a trail because the snow is thigh deep, but I quickly find a packed-down path that makes walking much easier. Someone is definitely making breakfast, because the aroma of coffee is strong when I get to the front steps. I smile at myself, thinking how bizarre my life is for me to know I'm supposed to enter a house I've never seen before. I'm wondering if I should bother to knock when the door opens.

I stare into a face with many of my features and a vivid version of my green eyes. But I'm not the spitting image of this woman, because she has straight dark hair, while mine is red and curly like my father's. A long-lost memory comes back to me, and I hear a voice singing in my mind. I realize why I know this woman.

"Are you my mother?"

"No, I'm your Aunt Patricia." She steps aside with a smile. "Come on in. I've been waiting for you."

PART 3

CHAPTER 21

Taylor

THE STAINED-WOOD DOOR opens, and a tall woman with jet-black hair invites me into the small cottage. She says she's my Aunt Patricia, and I enter. A fire crackles in the small open-space-style room that contains the kitchen as well as a living room. She says, "Go stand by the hearth, and I'll bring you some tea. I'm sure you're chilled to the bone."

I rub my hands together as I move toward the radiant heat from the burning wood. The December temperature in the winter wonderland of Maine is sub-zero today, and the cold has me shivering. Patricia comes to stand next to me, and I notice how thin she is compared to the women I've been surrounded by for the last few months.

I was pulled to come here this morning by a vision I couldn't ignore. I shifted into a bear and ran through the woods, guided by a dream-like version of the woman before me. I ask, "Why am I here?"

"You're a Veilleux stolen from us by the Le Roux."

I recall how the Veilleux kidnapped Sierra. The rescue mission was part of the reason I became a werebear. "I'm with the Le Roux voluntarily."

"That's because they managed to call you with a powerful spell, when you should have come to us instead. You're going to help me get the Veilleux heirs back where they belong." The teakettle whistles, and Patricia leaves my side to go to the kitchen.

The room swims before my eyes as I watch her walk away, and I shake my head to clear my vision. "But Victor kidnapped and raped Sierra for those children. Why do you think he should have them?"

A spoon clinks against a mug as Patricia stirs my tea. "You can't rape the willing. Sierra wanted my son as much as he wanted her. You know how the mate bond works."

The sight of Keith's dark hair over his eyes as he gazes down at me forms in my mind, and I smile as thinking about his love warms my insides. A flash of him on my kitchen floor confuses me again. He was hurt? *What happened?* I can't quite grasp the thread of thought.

"He bit her when she was mated to Keith."

"Oh, it wasn't Victor's doing. He has more honor than that. It happened with a little of my help. Sierra was supposed to have mated with him instead of Keith. So I remedied the situation." She hands me a cup of tea and takes a drink from hers.

She made Victor bite Sierra? I sip the scalding liquid in my cup in an effort to thaw my chilled limbs and sway a bit as the drink burns its way down my throat. Patricia offers me a fake smile. "You don't look so steady on your feet. Perhaps we should sit down."

She walks over to the couch and places herself on one end while I start toward the other. "Sierra took children that belong to the Veilleux. Surely you can see why the next leader of our clan should be raised by Victor?"

I frown down at my drink as I struggle with movement. I blink to help with my focus, because I don't feel completely here. It's as if a part of me is drifting away, and I drop down to the couch to ground myself. "But Sierra is the mother. They're going to... work out a c-custody..."

Patricia ignores me as she lifts a framed picture that's sitting on a side table. It's of her and someone I assume is her husband. She smoothes a finger over the image of the man. "Victor needs my help in so many ways." She glances back at me, and my blurred vision returns. "He just doesn't know it."

She sets the metal frame on the table with a thud and nods at my mug. "Finish your tea. We have a plan to discuss."

I WAKE TO calls in my mind that make the throbbing of my headache worse. Keith's voice rings loudly. *"Taylor! Taylor!"*

"Not so loud." I discover I'm in bear form and have a vague recollection that I had been running. I sit up on the rock I slept on. The rush of water is adding to my dis-

comfort, and I dive into the cold river to get to the shore and away from the noise.

"Thank God you've answered. Are you okay?"

My stomach is queasy, but the icy water in my mouth and nose provides some relief. *"I think so."*

The old Native American man who is a familiar vision these days appears to me. He says, *"You've suffered a concussion. Get home."*

I speak to Keith. *"I think I may have fallen and knocked myself out. It sure feels like it. I'm on my way home, and I'll be there soon."*

Brady's voice sounds. *"Do you need help? Where are you? We'll come."*

Jesus, like I need to be rescued. I'm not some weak woman. "No. I'm fine. I'll be there soon."

Running through the snow as a bear is wonderful. My steps are quick, and my strides are easy. The insulation of my fur keeps me warm, and I revel in the power of my animal form. The cold helps clear my head, and I get a sinking feeling I lost more than a few minutes to a nap. *What if the poison tea I was convinced was the cure to infertility left lasting damage?* No. It is the cure, and it's not poison. I'm *not* crazy.

When I arrive on our land, I find Keith pacing as a bear. He scans the horizon, and when his eyes find mine, he barrels toward me. He nuzzles me with his snout. *"I was so worried. Are you sure you're okay?"*

"I've got a killer headache, but I'm fine."

Bones crack as we both shift near the back door. The

moment we're inside, Keith pulls my nude body against his. "Don't ever scare me like that again. I couldn't live without you. It would kill me, too."

"I won't." I return his tight embrace while the odd sensation that I lost time again comes over me. I'm tempted to tell Keith, but that's the kind of thing that happens to people with split personalities, so I ignore it. I'm only one person, and a hungry one at that. "I'm not sure what happened exactly. I probably just hit my head." I suddenly remember our breakfast meeting and pull my head away to gaze up at Keith. "Oh, no! We're going to be late. You know how Donna hates that."

Keith steps back from me, and his brow knits in confusion as he takes my arms. "Taylor, it's the middle of the afternoon. We missed the meeting hours ago."

"Oh." *Whoa.* I chuckle to hide my shock. "That must have been some fall." I step away from him and turn to avoid his concerned gaze. "I'm going to take a shower and some ibuprofen."

"And I'm calling the doctor. I need to be sure you really are all right."

I stop when I get to the stairs and turn to face Keith. "Of course. But my guess is he'll tell me to take it easy for the next few days."

"Promise me you'll listen?"

The image of holding one of Sierra's children in my arms comes to me. "How about I spend time playing mom with some of the babies in this clan?"

"A doctor's visit would make me very happy. But

babysitting is also a good idea."

With each step I climb, I become convinced that babysitting is what I need to do.

CHAPTER 22

Carly

BRADY IS TAKING me to meet Kimi, and she'll explain how the binding ceremony will work. After Victor demanded custody of the children he sired with Sierra, the clans decided to compromise with shared custody. But it requires a magical bond to keep everyone honest. And alive. The spell will be cast over the prime and prima of each clan as well as over Sierra and Ashton. The Robichaux have agreed to be mediators in the process, and I'm grateful for their intervention. I know I can keep my cool around Victor, but I'm not so sure about Ashton and Brady.

We're in a developed suburb of Bangor, and it strikes me as odd. I imagined the Le Roux medicine woman lived in a small cabin set in a remote woodland area, so when I see the sign for Dancing Bear retirement community, I grin. "This is where Kimi lives?"

Brady's dark-blond hair is highlighted by sun filtering in through the window, and it gives off a false sense of warmth when I'm acutely aware of the bitter December temperature outside. "Did you expect a teepee?" he asks.

"No. But I did think she'd be a little more…" I shrug. "Mystical."

"Yes. Well, you don't look like a tattoo artist, do you?"

I hit his arm. "Are you calling me judgy?"

Brady grins at me. "No. Just teasing my wife."

We pull into a one of the plowed driveways that is just big enough to park the Hummer. When we get to the door, the petite Native American woman that greets us is wearing an oversized T-shirt that says, "Original American. No need to salute."

I smile at her when Brady introduces us, and she lets us in. Once we enter, I'm overcome by the aroma of chocolate chip cookies, and my mouth waters. Brady teases her, "What? No apple pie today?"

Kimi swats him in the stomach. "Careful, or I'll make you eat hot dogs." She glances at me. "You'll get a cookie if you learn your lesson well."

I nod and follow her like a good student. She leads us to a small living room that is decorated to reflect her heritage. I wander over to the beadwork hanging on the wall. The tiny beads are smooth under my fingers, and I say, "This is amazing."

"Thank you. I made it ages ago."

A folding table is set up with bowls of various herbs, and Kimi hands Brady a box of matches. He lights the candles around the room, and there is a comforting absence of words. The floor-to-ceiling drapes swish when the woman draws them shut.

She moves to the middle of the room and holds out her hands. Brady takes one, and I take the other. Her skin is cool and slippery, but her bony fingers grip mine tight as Brady grabs my other hand. Kimi says to Brady and me, "Close your eyes and imagine your life force as an electric current."

I wonder what this has to do with learning about the spell over Sierra's babies, but I do as I'm told and envision a white-hot source of power in my body. I picture that it's a rolling entity that emits heat in wisps of white. Kimi says, "Try to push it into me."

Now I visualize the ball of energy with a stream siphoning out of my fingers and into Kimi. It crackles through me, and I am startled that I can feel something. Kimi shudders as she grips my hand tighter. I begin to tremble as if I've just finished a tough workout and my muscles are fatigued. My instinct is to stop pushing the energy, but I only slow it down to a trickle.

I gasp when the sensation of my life force stream reverses and appears to be entering me. I let it flow until I feel normal again. Kimi lets out a sigh and releases our hands. I open my eyes and discover hers crinkled into slits as she chuckles. "There's a bit of magic in you."

"That's what that was?" I recall my past premonitions and odd sense of things I don't have a reason to know. But never before have I felt what just happened.

"Yes, and with training, you could use it. But for now, let's focus on what needs to be done to keep those babies safe."

Brady smiles at the news. "I'm not surprised. She's had me under her spell since the first time we met." He turns to Kimi and frowns. "Is this usual for werebear and I just haven't heard about it?"

"No. But I sensed something when I held Carly's hand earlier." She smiles as she taps her head. "Glad to know I haven't lost my touch."

"Will Tokala know she's a witch?" Brady asks. Tokala is the medicine man for the Veilleux.

I flinch. From what I know of clan history, witches are not friends of werebear. The idea of being one doesn't make me happy.

Kimi chuckles at my reaction. "I prefer 'gifted' to 'witch,' don't you?"

I grin back. "Yes. That's much better."

Returning her attention to Brady, she says, "He has no reason to suspect it and probably wouldn't reach out to find her power."

"Still. I'd rather assume the worst, because I don't trust the Veilleux or that man," says Brady.

I don't either, because he was the one behind the fertility tea that poisoned Taylor.

Kimi says, "We'll have to place Carly next to people that wouldn't know how to tap into her. I suggest Lily for the Veilleux and Richard or Marion from the Robichaux."

Brady shakes his head. "That's not good enough. Can you teach her how to hide her gift?"

Kimi frowns, "I can try. But she's new, and—"

"And we need it to happen." Brady's voice is stern, but I understand his concern. I don't want to take any chances with my best friend's children, either.

The old woman nods and glances at me. "You were given the magic for a reason. I'll work with you to make sure you can use it when it's time."

Her tone is ominous, and I would be a little freaked out if I had a normal life. But normal is so far in my past that I don't even bat an eye at the idea of learning some witchcraft. I nod and say, "Let's get the ceremony stuff sorted out first, and then we can work on me."

After Kimi walks us through how the protection spell will work, she sends Brady back home to take care of the babies so I can spend a few hours working with her. Sitting at her kitchen table, I feel right at home and imagine what a childhood with a mother might have been like. The aroma of onion adds to the delicious flavor of the soup she serves me.

Kimi asks, "Tell me about the strange things you discovered you could do as a child." She slurps soup from her spoon.

My mouth is full of the creamy mushroom dish, and I want to savor the tangy flavor instead of answering. But I swallow and answer, "I couldn't really do anything other than predict the future sometimes. And often I just knew things that couldn't be explained. I used to tell my father, and he'd get a strange look when I did. I stopped because it seemed to upset him. And now I realize he probably thought it was a werebear thing."

"Interesting. So he knew your mother was a skin walker." Kim tears off a piece of bread and stuffs her mouth with it.

I've never heard the term "skin walker," but it seems appropriate to think of it as something that happens to an animal instead of a human.

Kimi says, "Use your energy and push the salt over to me."

I tilt my head at Kimi. "I can't move things."

"Open your mind, Carly. You have more power than you know." She taps the shaker, and it thuds from the contact. "Try."

I stare at the salt and imagine my ball of fire streaming out and giving it a small shove. The shaker flies across the room and hits the wall before landing on the throw rug in front of the sink. "Whoa."

Kimi grins at me. "My doctor would be pleased; he's trying to get me to cut back. Push me the pepper instead."

This time I imagine a pinpoint-sized stream nudging the shaker, and the result is appropriate. "Wow. Is everything this easy to learn?"

"No. You have more control than most. I'm surprised you never stumbled on this power by accident."

I recall how handy it would have been if I had. "Maybe it was something that was dormant in me until I changed into a werebear."

"Could be." Kimi picks up her bowl and drinks the remains of her soup, and her lack of manners makes me stifle a giggle.

I do the same before standing to clear the table. "What else can I do with my gift?" Dishes clash in the sink, and I fill it with hot water.

"I don't know yet. Let's get a blocking spell to work first, and then we can play with your powers." Kimi nudges me over so she can get soap from under the sink. A stream of blue splashes into the water. "Tomorrow, you bring lunch. I'll go broke feeding you every day."

Every day? I try to hide my excitement over my newfound powers, but I can't help the grin that covers my face. Kimi hands me a sponge and winks at me as she says, "You've been in my dreams far too long. Maybe now I can get some sleep."

CHAPTER 23

Lily

RUNNING INTO ANNIE at the clothing store today was bittersweet. I should have guessed it might happen when we were both on neutral ground, and I'm glad it did. It was wonderful to see my friend again, but the information she gave me only confirmed my recent fears. My husband is evil. He held Sierra hostage to make her bear his children, and once she managed to escape, he rushed me into marriage.

When I arrived home from my shopping trip I was informed that Victor was bringing Tokala, our medicine man, to go over the custody spell he plans to cast in order to keep Victor's children safe under the Le Roux care. Funny, but I'm beginning to think it's the Veilleux that are the threat. Waiting in my study, I slam the teapot down a little too hard on the tray, causing the china to rattle.

My relationship with Victor is surrounded by deceit, and I have too many unanswered questions. The biggest is why did he need Sierra to be the mother of his children when he knew I was his true mate and would have gladly taken on the job? Is there something about her heritage that makes her a better mother for the next Veilleux heir? I lift my cup to my lips and blow on the steaming liquid.

Hot tea warms my mouth before I swallow it, and it occurs to me that maybe Sierra is of Veilleux descent, making the bloodline cleaner. I get up to go to the window and gaze out at the twinkling white lights strung among the trees that line our long driveway. I remember thinking they would look like my stairway to heaven when I returned home from evening events. But now they remind me of how easily I was fooled by the glamorous exterior of my new life and the charming deception of my true mate.

The headlights of the town car bounce along in the distance, and I mentally prepare myself to act as a loving prima. While I can't change the situation, I can certainly make sure my husband's children are safe under my care.

I make my way to Victor's den to ensure everything is ready for our meeting. A cool draft from the basement door makes me wrap my arms around myself as I walk by, and I frown, wondering if it's still locked. I tried to go down earlier in the month to find holiday decorations but couldn't get through. The decorations appeared soon afterward, and I wonder if maybe there's something down there I shouldn't see. The antique brass knob is cold in my hand when I twist it to no avail. There's a deadbolt keeping it shut, and my mind returns to imagining horrible things.

I press my ear to the wooden door to listen as if maybe someone is being kept prisoner. Carol's feet tap toward the hall, and I pull away before I'm caught and scurry to the den. I'm losing my mind! Victor couldn't possibly be keeping someone here against their will without me knowing it. I turn as Carol enters the room, asking, "Is there anything else I need to get for you?"

The heavy front door opens with a groan as I answer, "Everything looks great, thank you."

Victor's voice booms down the hallway when he sees me step out of the den. "There she is, my lovely wife. Come, darling, meet an old family friend. This is Tokala."

The Native American is dwarfed by the massive build of my husband, but when he takes my hand, the strength in his grip is anything but small. "It's a pleasure to meet you, Mrs. Veilleux." He smiles at me with a gaze that makes me feel as if I'm wearing a flimsy outfit and sharing too much.

Can he read my mind? I give my thoughts a quick shake, because I'm getting paranoid. I say, "Please, call me Lily."

I lead the men into Victor's den and offer them drinks. I pour the usual whiskey for Victor and sparkling water for Tokala and myself. I have no intention of being the least bit off my game around my husband.

Tokala eases back into an overstuffed chair and sets his drink down. He asks, "Lily, how are you adjusting to being the prima?"

"Fine I think. I'm enjoying the volunteer work quite a

bit." I turn to Victor. "What do you think? How am I doing?"

Victor seats himself next to me on the couch and places a hand on my knee. I fight the urge to pull away. "She's doing more than fine. The clan loves her."

Tokala nods the slightest bit and steeples his fingers over his mouth as he watches us, and I suddenly feel as if I'm in a therapist's office ready to share my shameful secrets. I lean against Victor as if the physical contact will show Tokala that I love my husband. "That's sweet of you to say. But the Veilleux are welcoming, and it's been quite easy."

The old man leans forward and says, "Let's talk about the spell. Shall we?"

I sit a little straighter as the ice in Victor's glass rattles when he takes a drink. He sighs in pleasure and then says, "Yes. I don't suppose there's a chance we can spell the Le Roux right out of the mix, is there?" My husband's laugh rumbles low in his throat, and I offer a smile at his humor.

Tokala's eyes are on me, and it's clear he's studying my reaction. He says, "No, and it's not in the best interest of those children. They should know their birth mother." His brown eyes are almost black, and something about his voice makes me think he knows more than he should. He turns his gaze to Victor. "After all, the spirits decided Sierra should bear your heir, so we must abide by their choice."

Victor says, "Very well. What do we need to do to

prepare for the ceremony?"

The medicine man walks us through the procedure and explains that the children's time will be split evenly between the two families. He states that if any harm comes to the either prime or the prima or Sierra or Ashton, the alpha abilities of the next heir of both clans will be thrown to the spirits to come back and land wherever the powers that be decide.

Victor stands and moves with the grace of a panther as he pours himself another drink. He says, "That's quite sobering news. Anyone else need something stronger than water?"

I think it's quite clever and ask, "If there wasn't a Veilleux heir, what would happen to the clan?"

"After the prime and prima died, it would dissolve, and members would have to petition another clan for acceptance."

Victor hands me a whiskey I didn't ask for. "Need this now?"

I say, "Thank you." I ask Tokala, "What happens if the alpha dies before the heir is determined?"

Tokala winks at me as if we share a private joke, and I fight the flush rising to my cheeks, because he can't know I've entertained the thought of killing my husband. "The prima runs the clan. I've heard she can even take on alpha tendencies if necessary."

His answer makes me uncomfortable, so I get back on the subject of custody. "So it seems we're stuck between a rock and a hard place with the children, aren't we?"

"For now." Tokala grins at us, and Victor lets out a belly laugh that makes me jump.

I watch the men chuckle and wait for them to explain what's so funny. When my husband recovers, he dabs at his eyes with a handkerchief and says to me, "There's more than one way to skin a cat, my darling."

I glance at Tokala, and he nods as his eyes bore into me like a warning. His gaze doesn't leave mine as he says, "Never underestimate the element of surprise."

CHAPTER 24

Sierra

I THINK I might be alone for the first time since I gave birth last month. Taylor came over this morning and offered to babysit, since she can't train anyone to fight while she recovers from her recent concussion. I called Donna in just to be safe and left the two able women with my kids. The coffee machine at Ink It gurgles as it fills my mug, and the lock of the front door clicks open as Carly enters the tattoo parlor.

With the holiday coming, our calendar is clear of appointments, but we decided to take walk-ins today. Most likely we'll hang out and talk about our babies while we enjoy the chance to sit without anyone needing our attention.

We'd moved on to our children when Annie bursts in the door, followed by a nearly nude man.

Her face is flushed from the cold. "Please tell me you have sweats big enough for this—this—" She huffs in a fit of anger. "Person. Bear." Annie's curls bounce wildly as she turns to look at him. "Whatever he is!"

The guy is even bigger than the Le Roux men and has hair so blond it's almost white. But his icy blue eyes capture your attention. They twinkle with amusement as he holds Annie's hat over his groin.

Carly says, "Ian probably has something."

She glances at me, and I don't want to leave before finding out what's going on. This guy has clearly got Annie flustered, and I'm sure it's good. But I know Carly will alpha order me if she has to, so I tilt my head toward Kick It and say, "Right this way."

Annie lets out a noise of disgust as I lead the guy away. He says, "I'm Tristan De Rozier, and apparently I've upset Miss Annie."

I lead him into Ian's office and turn to face him. I can't help but scan his body with my gaze. "I'm Sierra and married with children, so don't take this as a come-on, but I guess you've probably upset her in all the right ways."

He breaks into a grin that displays a mouthful of white teeth. "I'm sure I do. She may not know it yet, but I'm her true mate."

I snort. "Could you puff your chest out any farther? You're such a man." I toss a pair of sweat pants at Tristan. "Thank God, though. She needs you more than you could even know."

He throws the hat at me and steps into the pants without an ounce of modesty. Annie stomps her way around the corner toward us with Carly, and she says, "Please tell me you found something."

I hand Tristan a Kick It T-shirt and notice the sweats are tight over his massive thighs and... attributes. I wink at him just before she gets to us. "He's covered, but you should probably get him back to your place and let him run wild."

Annie glares at me, and I think she wants to stamp her foot. "You are no help at all." She turns to Tristan and sweeps her hand toward Carly. "This is Carly Le Roux, the prima."

He reaches for Carly's fingers. "It's a pleasure."

He kisses the top of her hand, and she says, "It's a pleasure to meet you, too, Tristan. We're thrilled to have you."

Annie rolls her eyes and says to him, "Come on. Hopefully your sister is waiting at home with your things."

Tristan raises his eyebrows at me as I cover my mouth with my hand in an effort to hide my snicker. He says, "I've got my orders. Nice to meet you, Sierra." He turns to Carly. "Mrs. Le Roux."

As they walk out, I speak in Carly's mind. *"True mate."*

Her laugh rings loud and clear before she says, *"That explains a lot. This should be entertaining."*

Carly goes over to the coffee station to make herself a cup and says, "I just realized we should have gone gift shopping today."

"I did all my shopping online. No way do I want to deal with the crowds." I grab candy-cane coffee creamer from the mini fridge and splash some in my mug.

"Good point. I only need the stocking stuffers for Brady, but I can get them tomorrow." We wander back to Ink It. "I have something kind of cool to tell you."

The aroma of mint wafts up as I sip my coffee, and she says, "I'm kind of a witch."

"Kind of? Aren't you either one or not?"

"Well, I prefer to call myself gifted, and yeah. I am one." She walks over to the couch to take a seat.

"That is pretty cool." I move to the chair opposite Carly. "What can you do?"

Carly nods her head toward the books on the table between us. "Watch."

I'm expecting a small fire or something, because she doesn't do anything but stare at the albums. Then I notice one rise above the pile and hover in the air. "Whoa."

It drops with a thump. "Neat, huh?"

"Can you fly one of your babies in the air to you in the middle of the night?"

Carly chuckles with me and says, "I haven't tried that yet. Right now I'm torturing Brady and Annie by clearing the table instead."

"I can just imagine. Break anything yet?"

"No. But by the way Annie freaks out so easily, I'm tempted."

As we laugh, someone pushes open the front door of the shop, and I glance over to see a dark-haired girl enter. "Hi there. Are you here for a tattoo?"

Carly asks, "Tori, right?" She pats the space next to

her on the couch.

"Yes." The visitor's zipper hums as she unzips her jacket and joins Carly on the sofa. She glances quickly at Carly's wrist and points. "I'm here for one of those."

I scoot to perch on the edge of the chair. She's one of us, and I'm anxious to induct her into my crazy sister-hood. "Do you know why?"

Tori's eyes are big as she says, "I'm not sure."

Carly asks, "You have a dream with this in it, don't you?"

"Yes. And it has a bear, too, so I thought it was a sign I should come to Orono. You know, because the university's team is the Black Bears." She slips out of her coat. "But the dream didn't go away."

Of course not. She's been called, and Donna's going to do what she can to get this girl hitched and pregnant by next summer.

I ask, "What does your guy look like?"

Tori's cheeks get pink with a flush. "Um. He's huge." She covers her face with her hands. "I mean, like, tall and—"

I interrupt her. "I'm sure he's big all over." I chuckle.

"Oh, God. That's not what I meant to say."

Carly grins at Tori and says, "Sierra and I used to get the same kind of dream. She's just teasing you."

"So you've been having this dream since last spring?" I ask.

"Yeah, and I can't fight it any longer. I need to get that tattoo before I go crazy."

Carly says, "Okay, but I have to warn you. The dreams don't stop until you also meet the guy."

"Oh." Tori bites her lip as she drops her gaze.

Poor thing is too shy to ask what she wants to know, so I help her out. "They're just as hot as in the dreams. Promise."

Tori frowns as she glances at me. "Why am I dreaming about him?"

"You've been called. Think of it as kind of like cosmic matchmaking. But don't worry. If you end up not liking the guy, you don't have to date him."

"So how do I meet him?"

I wink at Carly. "We can help you out with that. But first, let's give you a tattoo."

CHAPTER 25

Carly

ONE OF THE things Kimi and I are working on is my ability to sense true emotions from telepathic communications. As soon as I opened my mind to my magic, I discovered that I see colors in my head associated with the things people say. So it's no surprise that Annie's voice is laced with red when she sends a message from home.

"Isabelle is here, and she brought Tristan's clothes. And he just announced they're staying through the holiday. Of course I was polite about it and invited them to remain at our house. But that man!"

What's interesting is that her words are also mixed with purple, which is the color I've seen when Brady is sexually aroused. I wonder if she's figured out that Tristan is her true mate. I reply. *"Sexy, isn't he?"*

I chuckle to myself as I power down the laptop at Ink It, and Annie says, *"He sure thinks he is. But I find him annoying as hell."*

My sweet sister-in-law is in denial, because I know

how the true-mate attraction feels, and she's in for a wild ride with Tristan. I'm still grinning when Sierra comes out of the tattoo room with the garbage. We've decided to close early and get some last-minute Christmas shopping in after all. I wasn't above bribing her with the promise of coffee and cake at our favorite bakery.

"What's so funny?" she asks as she reaches for our coats on the hooks.

"Annie's all worked up about Tristan. It's cute." The nylon of my jacket is smooth to the touch, and my arm slips in quickly.

"He's more than cute. That guy is beyond hot. And did you see his cock? He might rival Keith at full mast."

"You'll have to tell Donna." I push the door open into the cold for us to exit.

Sierra giggles. "Poor Annie. She's in for a lifetime of teasing."

The lock clicks shut, and my keys jingle as I drop them into my purse. "Yup, and it makes me so happy for her."

"Me too. She deserves a steamy relationship. And boy oh boy, is she going to get it. Do you think—"

I hold up my hand to stop Sierra, because Donna's voice is faint in my head as if she's too far away to reach me. I can't make out the words or determine the meaning of the color surrounding them. It's a deep maroon that I haven't encountered yet. "It's Donna, but she's not clear." I call out to her mentally, but she doesn't reply.

"She's probably distracted. She's babysitting for me."

The sun is bright, making us squint at the reflection off the snowbanks that line the sidewalk.

"That makes sense. She might not have realized she was tapping into me." We're headed to a bath and beauty shop a block away so I can get stocking stuffers, and I decide I'll pick up something small for the De Rozier twins, too. I ask, "Do you think we should check on Donna?"

"No. We'd know if something was wrong. Taylor's there, too. She's still got an obsession with being a mother, and I guess she decided she needs to practice." Sierra shrugs. "I don't mind. It's nice to have time off." She links her arm in mine. "Can we get cake first?"

"No way. You'll ditch me before I get my errands done, and I need your help." We've reached the boutique, and I pull the door open for us. "Let's find some sexy bath salts for Annie and Tristan."

"Oh, good idea." Sierra stops and inhales the aroma of soaps and lotions. "Spicy—I think that fits what's ahead for them, don't you?"

I chuckle. "You're as bad as Donna."

Sierra winks at me. "Probably worse."

An hour later, we've managed to finish my shopping and are at the Cat's Meow. The French-inspired cafe is busy this afternoon, and the noise level is higher than usual. I sip a decadent hot drink made with real cream and imported chocolate. I recall the shopping trip Sierra and I took last year, which ended in a mall coffee shop.

I say, "This is a far cry from what our lives used to

be."

Sierra licks her fork, which is covered in cream cheese frosting from her carrot cake. "Um-hmm. Who'd have thought I'd be married to the love of my life and have triplets?"

"And me." Being in public means we can't talk about werebears, but I don't have to say anything more, because Sierra's been with me through just about everything that has happened since we decided to take our crazy road trip last spring.

Sierra reaches across the table and grabs my hand with a tight grip. "Promise me we're going to do this every year and that one day our children will roll their eyes at the things their ridiculous mothers say and do."

"Of course." I take her hand while I trace a finger along a flower on her lower arm and remember how I gave her the tattoo. It was the first of many.

"That one will always be my favorite. It reminds me of what a treasure you are, Carly. Thanks for being my best friend."

My eyes water, and I glance at the shiny gaze of the woman who is my best friend, too. She's been with me through the good and the bad, and she's never left my side. "Every girl should be lucky enough to have someone like you."

Sierra sniffs. "We're getting sappy in our old age." She breaks off another piece of cake, and before she bites, she asks, "What did you get Brady for Christmas?"

I'm about to answer when Donna's voice screams in

my head. *"Carly! Brady! Sierra's babies are gone! And I think Taylor took them."*

The shock must show on my face, because Sierra doesn't ask why when I throw a twenty on the table and say, *"We need to get out of here. Now."*

CHAPTER 26

Taylor

M Y PLAN STARTED off so well. Sierra jumped at the chance to get out of the house when I offered to babysit. For a moment, I thought there might be a problem when I discovered she had invited Donna to help me, but the reality was I needed the assistance. Three babies are a lot of work. When I got the chance, though, a sleeping pill in Donna's tea was a cinch to pull off. But I really should have kept her awake long enough to load the babies into her car. Because right now, I can't get the child seat to snap into place on the base.

How the hell does this thing work? I glance down at Jackson's blinking eyes. "Too bad you can't talk. I could really use your help." Plastic grinds as I jiggle the carrier around trying to find the right spot. A loud snap tells me when I do. "Finally!" I quickly load the other two kids and climb into the driver's seat of Donna's BMW. *Nice car.* I hope it can handle the back road to Patricia's cabin.

I glance at the huge bag full of diapers, formula, and clothes. I'm not sure if I got what is needed, but it'll have to do.

Inexperience with babies was almost my downfall. As soon as I got Donna to sleep, the children started wailing, and I realized they needed to eat. And that triggered three diaper changes, along with a change of clothing for some. Apparently not everyone can contain the velocity at which their contents decide to explode. Motherhood is no joke. By the time I was done, Donna had started to moan, and I wasn't sure how long I had before she woke up.

I flip on the radio, and loud rock music blares. "Shit!" I quickly turn down the volume and glance in the rear-view mirror to see if it bothered the babies. But the darn kids are all facing backward, so I take the lack of scream-ing as a good sign. "Sorry, guys, I think I just taught you your first swear word." I chuckle at the absurdity and scan the radio stations for a classical one to counteract my profanity.

A driver of another sedan waves as he passes, and I wave back as if I'm supposed to be taking Donna's grandchildren to a remote cabin in the woods. Donna's day is about to suck, but it can't be helped. Sierra's babies belong to the Veilleux, and Patricia and I are going to make sure they end up with Victor.

Snow flurries dance in the wind ahead of me. Anoth-er storm is coming, and I'm glad I managed to get on the road before the brunt of it hits. The route to Patricia's is engrained in my memory, but having never driven it, I pay careful attention to the side streets so I don't miss my turn.

As I get closer, the speed limit decreases, and the clear pavement becomes snow-covered dirt. I wince as Donna's BMW bounces over potholes. It's murder on her alignment, and I make a mental note to get that fixed for her later. Later? An uneasiness settles in me. *What the hell am I doing?* The traction is getting progressively worse, and my wheels slip, causing me to slow down to avoid fishtailing.

A horn blares, and I glance in my mirror to notice a large truck behind me. The lights flash on and off, so I slow down to pull over and let him pass. But when I stop, I realize the guy is still behind me.

I get out of the car to see what the man wants. He calls out to me as he walks in my direction. "Taylor?" A long gray ponytail hangs over his shoulder and rests on his chest, and his ear-flap hat with dangling braided yarn ties looks like it's decades old.

A tidal wave of fear mixes with that nagging feeling you have when you are about to do something stupid but can't stop. I blink and shake my head to clear my confusion. I say, "Yes, that's me."

"I'm Tokala. I'm here to get you up the road. Your car won't make it much farther."

"Oh, good. I'm afraid it's already having trouble."

"You've got three babies with you, right?" He smiles at me, making his eyes almost disappear in the wrinkled skin of his ancient face, and the previous fear grips my heart. Something's definitely not right.

Adrenaline surges in me, and I tense, preparing to protect myself. "Yes." As we make our way to Donna's car, my senses are on high alert. I'm afraid danger lurks in this man. I add, "I hope you know how car seats work, because these suckers are tricky."

He places a hand on my arm to stop me, and I'm about to make an offensive move when his touch makes my body tingle and relax. "Ten grandchildren. I'm a pro."

Oh my God. He's the man in my dreams. Relief washes over me, and as if fog has lifted, my purpose becomes clear. I know this man isn't dangerous. Between the two of us, we manage to get everything loaded into his truck and, within a mile, turn onto a road that appears to not have been plowed at all this season.

We descend a steep hill through woodlands, and Tokala says, "Good thing I packed the chains. I might need them to get back out." His voice barely registers, because I'm focused on the deja vu I feel as the trees thin out. I recall why when I remember the first time I came to this cottage. Only I remember it a vast meadow. Now I realize it's a lake and wonder how I could have possibly been so confused, considering I walked right beside it.

The cabin is off to the left, and we turn in that direction on a road that is barely visible. "You must know this by heart," I remark, "because I wouldn't be sure I was going the right way."

Tokala says, "Wouldn't matter so long as you made it to the cottage."

I suppose he's right. I turn around to check on the

babies in the back. They're all asleep and have no idea what an adventure they're on. When I face forward again, I notice Patricia exiting the house to greet us. She's bundled up and must have been watching so she could help get the children inside.

When we stop, Patricia barely takes notice of me and Tokala, and she pounces on the back door to get to the babies before my seatbelt clicks open. She coos when she removes one, and I realize this is the first time she's seen her grandchildren. I say, "That one is Justin. Jason is in the blue, and Jackson is wearing green."

The walkway to the cottage has been shoveled, and each adult carries a child into the house. I bring the diaper bag as well, and it thuds on the wooden floor when I drop it. A sense of completion makes me sigh. My mission was successful. I take in the cottage as the uneasy feeling comes over me again, and I frown.

Patricia nods in my direction and turns to Tokala. "Is she…?"

He mumbles, but I hear the words, "She's got a strong will."

What? The same relaxing warmth I felt before returns when Tokala takes my hands. "Come. You need some tea and a cozy fire."

I follow him and sit down, suddenly exhausted from the day's events. The sensation of floating above the couch is relaxing, and I'm almost asleep when Patricia hands me a warm mug. She says, "Drink this and then you can nap. You did well today, Taylor. Thank you."

CHAPTER 27

Lily

I'M ENGROSSED IN a romance novel when Victor's voice brings me back to reality. "Darling, I have the best news. I'll tell you all about it in the car, because you need to get ready quickly."

"What is it?" My e-reader clatters on the coffee table, and I swing my feet around to the floor.

"My mother has arranged to get the babies to us today, but we need to go to her." Victor lifts me up by my hands and gives me a kiss my body wants even though my head is reluctant.

Patricia. I knew her absence wouldn't be a permanent thing. Victor downgraded her to a small lake cabin he owns, and I ask, "Are we going to the cottage?"

"Yes. So dress appropriately. The road isn't always clear, and we may need to hike in."

Oh, God. "Sierra?"

"She's fine." Victor lifts my chin with a finger. His eyes look truthful. "I asked about her. The fact I care is a testament to you, darling. You make me a better person."

I give my husband a smile, but my mind races with the news. Patricia kidnapped the children, but she didn't kill Sierra. Victor releases me to leave, and I say, "I'll be up in a minute."

I bet good money Tokala has a spell in mind to keep them from Sierra forever. Fear for her grips my heart. After what my husband did to Sierra to bring those babies into the world, she sure doesn't deserve to have them stolen, too. But what can I do to fix this?

The rattle of dishes in the kitchen offers the answer. Carol. Paper rustles as I grab a sheet of stationery and scratch out a note to Francoise, the manager at the Cat's Meow. "Please contact Annie right away and tell her the shipment is at the cabin on Silver Lake." I'm sure Annie must know the Veilleux have a cabin there, and she'll understand what I'm trying to say.

Victor is upstairs, and I have to hurry, or he'll wonder what I'm doing. I take a deep breath to hide my panic as I walk to the kitchen. "Carol, I need you to do me a favor. This note should be delivered to Francoise at the Cat's Meow right away. Can you do that for me as soon as we leave, please?"

Carol wipes her hands on a tea towel. "Of course, Miss Lily." She takes the sealed envelope from me, and I have no doubt she's curious. Fortunately she's well trained, too, and she doesn't ask questions.

"Thank you. I appreciate it." The moment I'm out of sight, I jog to my room to get dressed.

Victor is pulling on wool socks and grins at me.

"We're getting an early Christmas present. Won't it be lovely to have babies for the holiday?"

I paste on my smile. "It will." I search my mind for something deliriously trivial to say. "I'll have to get them stockings. And presents. Oh goodness, I'm not prepared for this."

Victor walks over to me as I pull on jeans and takes me by my shoulders. "Darling Lily, they're babies. They'll never know." He brushes his lips with mine.

"Yes. But I will." I shake my head. "No matter. I'll deal with it all when we get back."

Victor chuckles. "I'm sure you will. You were born for this."

The words I was told in Colorado that convinced me I should come to Maine sound in my head. "You are destined to save a clan." I think to myself, *Oh, Victor, you have no idea what I was born to do.*

When I get to the garage, our black, oversized truck is already running. I climb up into a warm cab. I've barely shut the door before the gears clunk into reverse. "A bit excited, are we?" I offer up a chuckle.

Victor's face gleams with the joy of a boy on Christmas morning. "Partially. But the truth is, I'm not sure if we can trust my mother. I was quite cruel to her when I cut her off, and she might be up to something."

"True. But even though she's not my favorite person, she does want what's best for the clan. Surely she hasn't got evil intentions for the Veilleux heir."

Victor's large hand lands on my thigh, and I jump a

little. "You do ground me, my darling. Of course you're right. Even so, the sooner we get those babies while she's feeling charitable, the better."

While my husband is in a hurry, I want to buy the Le Roux time to stop something that most likely will be irreversible. "We should probably get diapers and formula. Have you asked Patricia if there's anything we need?"

Victor squeezes my leg before he removes his hand. "Always the planner. I'll ask, but I think she's probably fine."

I give him a minute to speak telepathically with Patricia. A storm has begun, and the soft thud of the windshield wipers beats a steady tempo. I gaze out at the snow-covered pine trees. The world looks dismal without any warm color to counter the white, black, and dark green. Before I realize what I'm doing, I sigh.

"Lily, are you having second thoughts about this?" Victor reaches for my hand and pulls it into his lap. "Talk to me. What's bothering you?"

"No. Gosh, no. I'm thrilled to become a mother. I—" I shift my body so I'm almost facing him and take a chance. "Poor Sierra. You really don't intend for her never to see her children again, do you?"

Victor's brow knits, and then he relaxes. "She can have more. The children are Veilleux and rightfully ours."

His callous words make me snap. "They're not puppies! They're her flesh and blood." I stop because I'm not sure how my outburst will be taken. "I'm sorry. I'm not thinking. It just touches me on a motherly level, imagining what it would be like if someone took my children away."

My husband takes a moment before he answers. "You're right. I know how distraught I am over not being with them. I'll arrange visitation rights."

Visitation rights. My stomach churns, and while he seems sincere, I wonder if he's just placating me, because I can't tell where the lies end and the truth begins. I imagine what we're about to do. I don't know if I can live with stealing another woman's children, even if my husband is the father. I sure hope Annie gets my message in time. I say, "Thank you. You always do the right thing."

"That's because you're my voice of reason."

I reach over and touch his arm. "Yes, and you're mine." I cross my fingers on my right hand and slide them under my leg as if the small action can actually work. "I'm sure everything will happen the way it's supposed to."

We've slowed down, and the blinker ticks to indicate a right turn. The road becomes more difficult to navigate, and Victor puts both hands on the wheel. Growing up in Colorado, I've done my fair share of driving in snowstorms, but I know better than to offer my help. Besides, maybe we'll get lucky and slide into a ditch that could delay us for a bit. An idea comes to me.

I place my hand high on Victor's thigh. "You know,

once we have three babies in the house, we may not get as much one-on-one time." My husband opens his legs, and I slide my hand closer to his crotch. I whisper, "I can be quick if you want to pull over."

Ever since I learned the evil truth about Victor, my head isn't into our lovemaking. But being true mates is a wonderful disguise, because my body can't help itself. Lust builds in my core as I rub my hand over rough denim, and my husband lets out a low growl. "Hold on. I know just the place."

The metal of his button is warm in my fingers when I release it, and I work the zipper down slowly. His lower abdomen is flexing as desire heats up and his erection hardens. My voice is husky when I say, "Don't crash." My seat belt retracts quickly when I unhook it, and the metal thuds against the door.

I lean over his lap and release his cock. Moisture oozes out the tip, and I swipe my tongue over it to taste his salty essence. I'm rewarded with a hiss. "Oh, God." The truck bumps over to the side, and I sit up to wait for him to park in what I guess is a private drive to a summer residence. Hope flickers as I pray we'll be stuck.

His seat hums as he moves it back as far as it will go, and I ask, "I take it that's a yes?"

Victor grabs my hips and yanks me underneath him as he lies on top of me to take my mouth in a kiss that tells me all I need to know. The weight of him is heavy, and I squirm underneath his body, realizing how easily he could overpower me if he wanted to. I shake the panic that's building and tug at his flannel shirt to reach under and scrape my nails lightly along his back.

My mate's hand is under my bra, and he pinches my nipple as I arch up, begging for more. I reach down and unfasten my jeans so I can wiggle them down. "God, I want you, Victor. I need you so bad."

He rises up on his knees to help me pull my pants below my knees before we work on his. Our boots keep us from removing our jeans completely, but it doesn't stop Victor from thrusting into me. "So warm and wet, darling." He settles himself all the way in and sighs as he holds still. "This is heaven."

This is hell. My thoughts turn to Sierra and imagine this is what it must have been like for her, too. Her body wanted my husband while her mind didn't. I want to focus on getting Victor to come as quickly as I can, because I don't want to think about my new reality. But I need this to last to give Annie time. I recall the first few weeks of marriage and how our passion was a symbol of true love. How blind I was. Now it seems to be a horrible twist of fate.

I squeeze my eyes shut and try to block out my thoughts to focus on the physical pleasure. My husband roars out his release as tears escape my eyes and roll down my face. Victor leans down and kisses them off my skin. "My darling, don't cry. Today will never change this for us. Our life is only going to get better. You'll see."

No, my darling. Everything is about to get worse. Much worse.

CHAPTER 28

Sierra

THIS CAN'T BE happening. My skin pricks with the urge to shift so I can run. But I wouldn't know where to start. *My children are gone!* I brace myself with my hand on the ceiling handle of Carly's Hummer as she takes a corner too fast. *Taylor was a spy for the Veilleux?*

Ashton's voice speaks in my head. *"I'll save them, Sierra. I promise."*

"Oh, Ash. I know you will. Stay safe."

Carly says, "We'll find them. I'll die before I let Victor steal your babies away from you."

I speak barely loud enough to hear, because I'm afraid if I say, it the words might come true. "Could he do that? It's not like he'd just disappear and leave his clan behind." The image of a jet plane and a Caribbean island come to mind. "Would he?"

"No. But Tokala—"

Oh shit. Magic. Now the tears come, and I don't bother to hold them back. "But you could fix it. You and Kimi, right?"

"Yes. I'm sure we could fix it, if it comes to that. But I'd rather not find out." Carly takes another corner so fast that the Hummer bounces sideways across the road.

"Where are we going?"

"I'm taking you home where you'll be safe."

"Home?" I shake my head. "Oh no. I'm not going to sit and wait for someone to save the day." Carly glances over at me, and I growl. "No fucking way."

She nods and turns her focus back to the road. "Fine. Annie just got a message from Lily, and she's positive Taylor took your children to a remote cabin the Veilleux own. It's on a lake, and—"

"Wait. We're trusting Lily now?" My hands clench into fists, and my breathing is barely keeping me from shifting.

"Yes. Annie does, and that means so do I." Carly's voice is dangerously close to being alpha, and I almost wish she would order me so I'd feel the confidence of following my leader. She continues, "You, Annie, and I are going to drive as close as we can undetected so there's a car nearby once we get the babies."

I snap at her. "We're fucking werebear, and we're going to use a car?"

She reaches over and places a hand on my arm. "The triplets can't survive being carried by a bear for miles in this storm."

"Oh. Shit." I'm losing it. God, I want Ashton to hold me and tell me everything's going to be all right. But I know he's out there running the rescue mission, and he can't deal with his needy wife. "Okay, go on."

Carly slides us around the corner to her driveway, and the bark of a tree whizzes by my window as we just miss it. "Ashton, Brady, and the team are going to get into the building and remove the babies."

"And what do we do?"

"Well. Annie was going to stay with the car because I need to go along with Kimi in case—" She pauses. "You know." She slams the car into park but leaves it running as she gets out.

I jog behind her to the house. "Yeah, in case Tokala puts the hex on my children so they will combust or something if they come near me."

Annie opens the door and pulls me into a big hug as Carly ducks by her. "Sierra, I'm so sorry. We're going to fix this."

Everyone keeps saying that. I bite my lip to keep from crying and nod. A model-gorgeous girl is in the living room behind her, and I guess it's Tristan's sister, Isabelle. Her blue eyes are huge in porcelain skin framed by straight hair that is more white than blond. She watches us as Annie releases me and turns to her to say, "This is Isabelle. She's going to stay with you in case Victor has plans for you, too."

Isabelle sticks out her hand, and I notice how much bigger it is than mine. She says, "I kick ass and like it." She squeezes me hard enough that my bones grind together.

"I don't doubt that for a second, but I'm not staying."

Carly has returned and tosses me a backpack. "Sierra's coming with us and will stay with the car." I open my mouth, and Carly glares at me. I shut up before I get alpha ordered, because I don't intend to sit this one out. She continues speaking to Annie. "That way you can join me and watch my back so we don't have to call someone from the team."

Isabelle says, "I'm coming, too. I'll stay with Sierra."

Carly is already walking toward the door and says, "Fine. Let's go."

Annie has gone to the kitchen and comes running back to throw a half-zipped bag at Isabelle, who catches it in one hand as if it's a ball instead of a heavy pack. When we get to the Hummer, I scramble into the back and let Annie sit up front to navigate.

Annie gives Carly directions and turns to me to say, "I got a call from Francoise at the Cat's Meow. Quite clever of Lily, by the way." Annie grabs onto the headrest to steady herself as Carly swerves around a car to pass it. "Francois is a wholesale contact she acquired for us, and he would have no reason to know that Lily and I aren't still working together. The note said that the shipment was at the lake house."

Carly slides the Hummer back into our lane, narrowly missing the oncoming car that's blaring its horn. Isabelle mutters next to me, "Black bear are crazy."

Annie doesn't even turn around to see what's happening but continues. "It wasn't hard for me to figure out that she meant the babies are at the Veilleux's summer cottage on Silver Lake."

"Annie!" yells Carly. "Where's the road?"

Annie whips around and says, "Around this corner and on the left. And you might want to slow down for it."

She doesn't, and my body slams into the side of the car. Pain in my shoulder makes me wince; so much for seat belts. Annie says, "This road is parallel to the one that leads to the cabin. When we see the lake, we should pull over."

"So you and Carly are going to sneak in through the woods?" I ask.

"Yes. Between the two of us, we'll carry the babies back to the car. There are warm blankets and formula in my bag."

I reach for it on the floor, and the zipper hums as I open the canvas duffle. I haven't let myself go there yet, but the moment I see the bottles, my sweet children's faces come to mind. Justin's little curls that barely cover his scalp, Jackson's perfect heart-shaped lips when he's sleeping, and the powerful kick of Jason's that Ashton is sure means he'll be a warrior. The sob I was containing escapes with a gasp, and the floodgates to my tears open.

Carly has stopped the car and turns to me. "We're going to save them. Stay strong, and I'll message you as soon as Annie and I are on our way back."

I nod. I glance over at Isabelle. I'm sure she's wondering what she stepped into, and I offer her a weak smile. "I promise I'm not always this much of a drama queen."

Carly and Annie's doors groan open, and they get

out. Carly give me one last look. "I won't fail you, Sierra."

Isabelle and I watch the women attach snowshoes and make their way into the forest. They aren't shifting because they need to be human to carry my children back to the car, and it's faster to stay that way instead of shifting and dealing with changing in and out of winter gear. The moment they're out of sight, I kneel up in my seat to reach into the back. I grab the extra pair of snowshoes and say, "I'm going."

Isabelle says, "I would, too. I'll watch the car." She pulls the blankets out of the duffle bag. "I'll be ready when you get back."

"Thank you." *For believing my children will be saved and for knowing why I have to do this.*

CHAPTER 29

Carly

ANNIE AND I don't speak as we trudge through deep snow toward the Veilleux cabin. A twig snaps as I pull branches out of the way, and I slow down to be quieter. We should have the element of surprise, since the Veilleux can't know that Lily sent us a message.

When the lake appears, I stop. Wind blows, freezing my nose with its icy bite. Annie communicates with me as she points her finger. *"The cottage is right over there."*

A sleek black truck that I guess is Victor's is parked behind an older one that has seen better days. Poor Patricia really was knocked down a peg or two when Lily became prima. The plan is for us to watch for the rescue team to enter and secure the area. I message the warriors. *"Annie and I are in place."*

Ashton's order comes to me, too. *"On three. One, two, three!"*

Part of me expects to see the door crash down and windows break, but that's not the way Ashton does things. He's already disarmed the Veilleux's perimeter

191

guards, and I imagine his team members are popping up from random places in the house to take their prisoners. Within seconds Brady's voice comes to me. *"Now, Carly."*

Annie and I race through the woods toward the cabin. With a quick yank of my straps, my snowshoes are off, and my feet thump up the stairs while Annie follows me. The wooden door slams against the wall as I shove it open, and the first thing I see is an old man that must be Tokala. Ian holds his arms behind his back, but fear grips my heart when I notice his eyes. They're glowing slightly, and I glance to see where his gaze is directed.

Kimi is standing with her hand in the air, her mouth moving in silent chanting. I want to ask how I can help but realize I can tap into her mind. I focus on her thoughts as I scan the room for the babies. Patricia and Lily are each being held by a warrior, while Ashton has Victor. Keith is with Taylor, and the children are in their car seat carriers, dressed to go outside.

Sure that my help is needed most with Kimi, I call up my powers and begin to siphon white-hot light to our medicine woman. I must be the boost she needs, because Tokala slumps as if he's unconscious. I ask Kimi, *"What did you do?"*

"Put him out of commission for a few minutes. Thanks for the help."

Victor growls, and I fear he's going to shift, but I know Ashton will, too, if necessary. Victor says, "You won't get away with this. These children are mine."

Sierra's voice is behind me. "They're mine, too." She

comes to stand next to me and asks, "Can we kill him?"

Before anyone can answer, Taylor speaks to me tele-pathically. *"No. There will never be peace if you do."* Black wisps surround her words, and it chills the blood in my veins. She's possessed.

I say, "Wait." I walk toward Taylor. She's on the couch next to Keith, and I speak to him telepathically. *"Restrain her. Something's not right."* Taylor grunts when Keith pulls her arms behind her back and lifts her to stand. She glares at me.

I then say, *"Kimi, Taylor's words are black. I need your help."*

"Push the evil away from her."

My power rolls inside me, and I channel a trickle to-ward the words I saw as if I'm blowing the dust off them. "Taylor, I'm going to fix this. Hold on." Sweat trickles down the back of my neck as I stare into her eyes.

Taylor's voice in my mind is weak. *"Help me, Carly."* But then her eyes turn dark, and she stomps on Keith's foot, disarming him for a second to step away. When she does, the sensation of my magic being sucked out of my body makes me gasp for air. Taylor opens her mouth to speak, but she doesn't get the chance before her body is propelled across the room and slammed against the wall with a loud splat.

Keith screams, "Taylor!" as he races to her broken body.

Did I do that? A cackling laugh from Tokala draws my attention, and he grins at me as he says, "She was lost to you anyway. I sold her soul to get what we needed. Thanks for helping me finish the job."

Oh, God. "Keith?"

His eyes are wide when he looks toward me. Crimson fluid streaks his face and covers his clothes. A tear rolls down his cheek, leaving a trail in Taylor's blood along the way. "She's dead."

Kimi hisses, "Tokala killed her." She lifts both her hands, and sparks shoot from her fingers straight toward him. They don't get there, though, because he blocks them with an invisible wall that makes them shoot through the floor. Kimi reaches into my mind. *"Fuel me."*

I turn my focus inward to my power and am just about to throw it to Kimi when Tokala vanishes as if he has gone with the magic that burned through the floor.

Ian says, "What the hell?" He glances around the room. "Where did he go?"

There's a hole the size of a person in the floor, and the smoke curling up from the edges smells of charred wood. Kimi says, "Where evil resides."

A roar makes the walls shudder, and I turn to see Victor shifting as he lunges toward Sierra, who's blocking the door as if she's backing out of the cabin. She has two of the babies, and her mouth sets in steely determination to fight. A wet swish sounds, and I watch Victor fall to his knees. Lily screams.

Victor's form returns to human, and he lands on his hands, gasping. Ashton yanks a knife out of his back, and the suction sound turns my stomach as I watch blood drip from the blade. His voice is cold when he looks at Brady. "You sure I can't kill him?"

Brady says, "No." He kneels down in front of Victor and growls. "He's going to die a slow, painful death this way."

Victor shakes his head, and his voice is raspy as he rolls to his side. "I wasn't going to hurt her." Blood is pooling around his body, and he's fading fast. "Tokala—" Victor coughs. "Sierra—"

A guard walks in the door with an arm across Tokala's chest and a knife at his throat. A black mist hovers around the old man. "He's right. This guy was about to capture Sierra. But his alpha must have blocked it, because his magic is no good."

Sierra hands the car carriers to a warrior and walks over to kneel in front of Victor. Brady tries to pull her to her feet. "Sierra—"

She shakes him off and touches Victor's arm. "You were going to save me?"

Lily is screaming to be let go, and I strain to hear what Victor says as he looks up at Sierra. "I'm sorry. Take good care of our children." His eyes flutter shut.

Sierra takes his hand and gives it a squeeze while tears stream down her face. She stands and says to Ashton, "Please... put him out of his misery."

Lily struggles to get free from her captor as she wails, "Please! I need to be with him. Let me go!"

Brady nods at the guard, and he releases her. Lily falls to her knees in front of Victor and pulls him up into her arms. "Don't leave me!"

Victor regains consciousness and grabs onto Lily as if he can take her wherever he's going. "My darling, I'm so sorry I failed you—" He squeezes her so tightly that they appear to merge into one. Lily's shirt is soaked black, and flecks of blood dot her face. He coughs, and I realize Victor is hacking up blood.

"No! Don't you dare leave me, Victor. I love you!"

Victor groans. "You made me the man I was... meant to be. I'll love. You. Forever." The last word is barely a whisper as his head falls and his body goes limp.

"No!" Lily sobs as she rocks with Victor's body in her arms. "No. No. *No*." She pushes the hair out of his face and whispers, "I'll love you forever, too."

Keith's quiet sobs float into my awareness, and anger surges in me. I glance at Kimi and nod my head toward Tokala. "What can we do about him?"

"I got this. Lend me some power."

Lily says, "No." She stands up and throws back her shoulders. Strands of hair have fallen out of her ponytail, and the elastic tie sags at the base of her neck. Her voice rings true. "I've got this." She walks over to Tokala, and even though her hands are shaking by her sides, she speaks with authority when she says, "As prima of the Veilleux clan, I proclaim you fired. Never set foot on Veilleux land again."

Kimi says, "Damn. That was better than any spell I could have cast. He's an untouchable now that a clan has denounced him."

Lily's boots beat a slow, steady beat as she walks across the room, leaving maroon footprints in her wake. She's covered in Victor's blood, and mascara is streaked on her face, but she appears as powerful as an alpha. She stops in front of Patricia. "I believe I can denounce you too. But I won't." She looks Patricia up and down slowly, disgusted, and lets out a low growl. "Don't make me regret giving you a chance to change." She nods at Patricia's guard, and he lets the woman go.

Patricia rubs her arms as she walks over to Victor's body. She lowers herself to the floor and stares at him in shock.

Keith is cradling Taylor's shattered body, and it's then that feeling returns to my heart as I imagine the pain of losing a true mate.

Lily then turns to Sierra and me. Her face is stone cold, but pain flickers in her gaze. "I would like for us to arrange equal custody. The children should know their birthright." She glances at Sierra. "And their birth mother." Brady comes up beside me as Lily steps forward. She reaches out both of her bloodstained hands. "I call a truce between the Veilleux and Le Roux."

Brady and I each take one of her hands. Brady says, "Truce." And I echo him.

Lily asks, "Would you like to perform a spell to ensure everyone's safety?"

I'm amazed at her logical thinking, considering she just lost the love of her life. I shake my head. "No. I trust you, Lily."

Sierra says, "Me too." She steps close to Lily and gives her a hug. "I'm so sorry."

Lily pulls away as if Sierra's touch might break her fragile exterior. "Me too. Now get those babies home. We can make arrangements tomorrow."

She directs her attention to Brady and me. "Let this be the beginning of a peaceful existence for the Northeast Black Bear Kingdom."

While Lily is not an alpha, she is now the official leader of the Veilleux. She will remain in her position until one of Sierra's children becomes an alpha and is a legal adult, and the prima will remain in position until the alpha chooses a wife. I look into her eyes with pride. "Yes. It will be an honor to serve on the council with you, Lily Wilson Veilleux."

I recall the shy, naïve girl I met at the motel in Colorado. Now Lily is a powerful leader who was called to save a clan. I watch Annie reach out for Lily, but the gesture is thwarted as Lily shakes her head and moves away.

Keith has carried Taylor's body out of the cabin, and I glance over at Victor and a crying Patricia. It's hard not to have sympathy for her as I try to fathom the pain of losing a child.

Brady takes my arm. "Mrs. Le Roux. I think it's time to get home to our family. I need to be close to them right now."

I lean against my strong husband. "Yes. I agree." I picture my sweet babies in my mind, and there's nothing

I want more than to be snuggling with them.

When we step outside, I discover the storm has let up. Someone must have found Isabelle, because our Hummer is parked in the driveway, and she's behind the wheel, waiting for us. As we get to the car, the sun breaks free from the clouds and shines down, making the snow sparkle with the promise of a fresh start.

CHAPTER 30

Lily

THE DAY AFTER a winter storm can be deceiving. I gaze out at the bluebird sky and bright sunlight glistening on the vast expanse of snow that covers the grounds of the Veilleux mansion. My mansion now. I push my way out the door and descend the marble stairs that are meticulously maintained by staff. I don't bother to watch my step because I know they're clear.

While the day's appearance is cheerful, the temperature hovers near zero, and the strong winds bite at my face as I make my way through the snow. I break a trail that will ruin the perfect blanket of white I see through my study window. It will remain a scar that fades over the winter as more snow falls until eventually it will disappear.

I lift my face to the sun and notice my eyelashes are frozen with crystals of moisture from my tears. I wipe a drop off my face and watch the residue freeze into a thin layer across my leather glove. I'll allow myself this one time to cry during the day, but then it must stop. The

Veilleux need me to be a strong leader in Victor's absence, and I'm determined to make him proud. My nights can be time for my sorrow.

Snow swishes around my legs as I continue to the perimeter of the lawn and walk along the edge of the forest. Movement makes me glance at the guard, who lowers his head as I go by. He's trained to speak to me only when necessary, and I've never bothered to change that ritual with the men that offer me invisible protection. I'll need to change that but not today. I suspect he's in mourning, too.

When I get to the gardens behind the house, I trudge over to a bench. I pack down the snow with my bottom when I sit on it. The tips of my fingers are cold in my fashionable gloves, and I slip them out of their casings to hold my hands in fists to ward off the chill. My husband and true mate is gone. I gaze past the yard to the forest and let reality sink in. All of this is mine now. I own thousands of acres of land, a profitable paper mill, a few houses, and hundreds of luxury items.

A chuckle escapes me. I have more than I ever wanted when it comes to material goods, but I don't have the one thing that ensured happiness. Victor was *changing*. My laugh becomes uncontrollable, as if I'm giggling with a girlfriend, until it gives way to loud sobs. I lie down on the bench and curl up my legs as my body shakes with my cries. Snow is so cold on my face that it hurts, but I don't bother to move as I let my anguish take over.

When I'm finished, I sit up, my shivering so violent

that I realize I need to get inside before I get hypothermia. I head toward the back door that leads to a storage room that houses cleaning supplies, laundry, and the pantry. It's Carol's domain, and I startle her when I enter.

"Goodness, Miss Lily." She frowns as I pull off my gloves and rub my hands together. "You've got frostbite on your cheek."

"Oh. It's colder out there than I expected." I reach up to touch my face, and while my fingers feel the skin, my cheek has no sensation where it's frozen. I hold the warmth of my hand on it until feeling returns.

"I've got soup on the stove if you'd like some."

I shake my head because I have no appetite.

"Miss Lily, you need to try. You've got a long day ahead, and you'll need protein."

She's right. I'm meeting Patricia at the funeral home this afternoon to make arrangements, and Victor's right-hand man Harold will be there. They both need to see I'm in control, and it's going to be a struggle to remain strong. I'm going to need my own right hand now. "Okay. I'm going to go change and will be down in a few minutes."

As Carol turns to walk away, I stop her. "Carol, wait." This woman is someone I would have liked to be my mother and the one person in the Veilleux clan I trust.

She turns back to give me her attention, and I say, "You know almost everything that goes on in this house. How would you feel about becoming my personal assistant?"

She reaches out her hands and takes a hold of mine. The warmth soothes the burning cold of my fingers. "I'd be honored."

THOMAS HOLDS OUT his hand to help me out of the town car. I climb out and gaze at the historic white home-turned-funeral parlor. I pause for a moment and take a deep breath. He asks, "Would you like me to come in with you, Miss Lily?"

I recall how he's been a solid presence at many of my difficult meetings and situations, and having him with me will be comforting. I'm also aware that he spent years driving Victor, and he's lost an important person in his life, too. It makes sense that he should be a part of my husband's final journey. I hold out my arm. "Yes, Thomas. I think Victor would like that."

A man in a black suit greets us when we enter. His voice is low and quite the way one expects a funeral director to be. "Mrs. Veilleux, I'm Martin Peabody." He holds out a hand for me to shake, and when I do, it's startlingly cool. "Right this way."

He leads us to a small office with plush chairs set across from a plain, dark wooden desk. We're directed, to sit and Mr. Peabody moves behind the desk. He pinches his slacks at his thighs before he lowers himself into a chair and says, "I know this is a trying time for you, and I'll direct you through the process as quickly as I can."

I say, "The elder Mrs. Veilleux will be joining us, and

I would like to wait until she arrives, if you don't mind."

"Of course." He sweeps his hand across the desk. "Please browse through the catalogues while you wait."

I pick up one for caskets and leaf through. This ritual seems ridiculous to me. I'm about to spend thousands of dollars to encase my husband's body in a lavish box to buried in the ground. I make a note to leave a will that says I want to be cremated and have my ashes thrown to the wind.

Footsteps announce Patricia's arrival, and I turn to the doorway to greet her. She's dressed in black like I am, but she also has a black veil over her face. I mentally roll my eyes at the drama. It's going to be hard to bite my tongue, but I'm determined to be gracious to Victor's grieving mother. Harold is with her and guides her to a chair before he seats himself between us.

I lean over Harold to speak to her. "Patricia. We haven't begun. I wanted to wait for you."

She nods in an answer. I hand her the book of caskets. "Would you like to choose?"

Patricia holds her hand up in a stop motion as if she's dismissing me and says to Martin, "We'll take the best you have in a mahogany with burgundy silk. The announcements should be done in Old English script, and the funeral should be early afternoon." She turns to me and says, "The ceremony following is to be held at the Jefferson Manor. The food should be heavy, and let the alcohol flow freely. Spare no expense. My son deserves the best."

While I'm tempted to assert my power, there's no need in front of Thomas and Harold, so I agree. "Thank you, Patricia. You've made this very easy for me, and I'm grateful."

She lets out a low noise of contempt. "It was necessary. I couldn't trust you to know the proper etiquette for this."

"Really?" I lean over and lower my voice to mimic Victor's alpha tone. "Whatever am I going to do when you die?"

CHAPTER 31

Carly

BRIGHTLY COLORED WRAPPING paper rustles as Annie crushes it into a large box. I don't think I could count the number of presents that were under our Christmas tree this morning. I scan the piles of gifts beside each family member and our guests. My gaze stops when it connects with Brady's. His hair is sticking up, and he needs a shave. He says, "Merry Christmas, Mrs. Le Roux."

I curl my legs up under me and wrap my hand around my coffee mug. I inhale the scent of cinnamon that tells me Annie has something delicious in the oven. "Merry Christmas, Mr. Le Roux." Audrey lets out a squeal, and Donna hands her a squeaky toy Santa brought. Annie has gone to the kitchen to check on the breakfast that Tristan and Isabelle insisted on making, and her exclamation carries to us. "Tristan!"

Donna looks up from the babies and winks at me. "Think he just pinched her butt?"

I chuckle as Brady gets up to come sit next to me, and

I remember first meeting Tristan at Ink It a couple days ago. It feels like it's been months considering all that's changed. "He says he's her true mate."

Brady says, "I hope he's right. She deserves another one." His face clouds over, and I guess he's thinking about his best friend Keith losing Taylor. Keith's a regular at the Le Roux house for holidays but declined the invitation for dinner later today. I don't blame him.

I reach over and take Brady's hand as I swallow the lump in my throat. I imagine Ian is having a hard time, too, since they were business partners and he was Taylor's closest friend. "Have you talked to Ian?"

"Yeah, he's kicking himself for not killing Tokala when he had the chance."

"Oh, Brady, nobody expected that to happen. Who could have known magic would kill her?" I snuggle into the crook of his arm.

"I know. But we all find ways to torture ourselves over the ones we love." I think my husband's words aren't just about Ian when he glances at his mother.

I say, "Sierra told me she spoke with Lily." I grin, watching Everett rock on all fours as he tries to figure out how to crawl. "Lily's going to spend time with Sierra and Annie next week before she takes the children for her week of custody."

Donna glances up at me, and I think it's guilt that crosses her face before she asks, "How's Sierra doing with that?"

My mother-in-law has to figure out how to live with

the shame of being tricked by the evil that took over Taylor and allowed the kidnapping of Sierra's children. It was a blow to her ego no matter how much we try to convince her it could have happened to any one of us. I say, "Amazingly well. The first time is going to be difficult, but Lily is understanding, and I'm sure it will get easier."

"Lily surprised me," says Brady. "She sure didn't seem like a leader when we first met her."

I glance at the calmest of my children, Elliot, as he manages a slow creep across the floor. "Sometimes it's the quiet ones that exhibit the greatest strength."

Donna says, "It will be interesting to see who she picks to sit with her on the council."

I recall my first prima luncheon with Patricia and Donna's dislike for the woman. "Well, it sure won't be Patricia. You would have liked the way Lily spoke to her."

Isabelle comes in from the kitchen and plops herself down on the floor beside the babies with a sigh. "I'm no longer needed in the kitchen." She scoops up Connell and holds him above her head to lower him while she makes a noise.

Donna asks, "Why's that?"

Isabelle places my son on her lap and waggles her eyebrows. "Too many cooks in the kitchen."

I grin. "What do you think about Tristan and Annie?"

"I think Tristan has found a good reason for our clan to move here." She tilts her head at Brady and me. "Annie's a nice match for my brother, and we're lucky to already have the next De Rozier alpha."

Brady stiffens. "You do?"

"Oh, yes. Tristan's got triplets too. His wife left us a couple years ago." She shrugs. "Big scandal, but it's not my story to tell. You'll have to pry it out of Tristan after a few glasses of wine."

I frown. I'm not sure what to make of Isabelle. She was quick to adapt the other day when the rescue mission went down, and I know she's a fierce warrior. But what does she need from us to be happy? Because she seems quite willing to move here, too. A vision of Isabelle in a barely-there bikini makes me grin, imagining that summer's going to feel unbearable to the polar bear clan, and nudity might become a thing we need to deal with.

I get up from the couch, and my mug thumps on the coffee table. I'm still in my pajamas, so I say, "I'm going to get changed before Sierra and Ashton get here."

When I return to my family, Sierra and Ashton have just gotten settled. I hug them both as we exchange holiday greetings. Sierra's boys are all asleep, and she's moved them to the bassinets my kids have outgrown. I watch as Ashton wraps his arm around her waist and they gaze down at their babies.

Tristan enters the room with a plate of pastries. "Breakfast will be ready in five." The dish clatters on the table and he adds, "I brought you Annie's bear claws while you wait."

Sierra taunts him, "Annie's made you her errand boy?"

Tristan flashes a sly smile. "Annie's trying to resist my sex appeal. She has to take a break every now and then." He rolls his eyes to the sky and sighs. "It's tough being this hot."

Sierra and I chuckle as he returns to the kitchen, and she says, "I like that guy."

"Me too." I wonder what the De Rozier twins will bring to our clan and welcome the chance to find out. The thought makes me smile to myself at how I've grown to love a challenge. I reach for a pastry.

To think, less than a year ago, Sierra and I were dreaming about sexy men, bears, and a new life in Maine. With two fresh tattoos calling us, we chased adventure with a road trip that would change our lives. I sink my teeth into the bear claw and smile when the sweet flavor pleases my taste buds. *And what an adventure it's been.*

The End

More By the Bear
by V. Vaughn

Called by the Bear – Book 1
Called by the Bear – Book 2
Called by the Bear – Book 3

Tempted by the Bear – Book 1
Tempted by the Bear – Book 2
Tempted by the Bear – Book 3

Rocked by the Bear – The Lindquists
Rocked by the Bear – The Vachons

Desired by the Bear – Book 1
Desired by the Bear – Book 2
Desired by the Bear – Book 3

Coming 2017
Loved by the Bear Book 1,2 & 3

V. Vaughn also writes contemporary romance as
Violet Vaughn. Learn more at www.violetvaughn.com

Made in the USA
Coppell, TX
03 September 2020